MW01277404

THE SECRET ADMIRER

THE SECRET ADMIRER

•

Annette Mahon

AVALON BOOKS
NEW YORK

Library of Congress Catalog Card Number: 2001088053
ISBN 0-8034-9484-X

Published by Thomas Bouregy & Co., Inc.
160 Madison Avenue, New York, NY 10016

PRINTED IN THE UNITED STATES OF AMERICA
ON ACID-FREE PAPER
BY HADDON CRAFTSMEN, BLOOMSBURG, PENNSYLVANIA

For my sisters, Janet and Mari,
for their continuing support and constant enthusiasm.

Prologue

Christmas music blared, conversation hummed, food disappeared from the tables faster than it could be replaced. It was a great party. The whole town of Malino, Hawaii, was there, plus people who'd moved away years ago and returned especially for the annual holiday pot-luck. Emma Lindsey leaned her head close to Matt Correa's chest, attempting to better hear what he was saying.

"Just look at you two." Emma's cousin Ray passed by them, a beer in one hand. He slapped Matt on the back with the other. "When are you two gonna get hitched?"

Emma's eyes widened. She would have met Ray's remark with indignant words, but he'd already forgotten them, moving along to another group.

She turned back to Matt, shrugging her slim shoulders. Instead of the incredulous humor she expected to find in his face, his eyes were solemn, staring down at her in serious contemplation.

"Where do you suppose he came up with *that* idea?" She tried to force some laughter, with little success. "Everyone knows we're friends. And neighbors. We don't *date*."

Matt's lips tipped up at one corner. "We're here tonight."

"Oh, Matt." She waved her hand at him, the way one might swat at a bothersome fly. "You know we just came together. Mom came with us, for gosh sakes. That's not a *date* date. We were both coming to the same place, so we drove over together."

Matt frowned. "You make it sound like car-pooling."

Emma smiled in triumph. "See? That's what *friends* do. They share rides and car-pool."

Emma had barely uttered the last word, when her Aunty Joy approached. A tall woman whose appearance reflected her Hawaiian heritage, she held a large plate of coconut candies in both hands and was urging them on everyone.

"Have some, Emma, Matt. I made them just before I left for the party, so they plenty fresh." Then she tweaked Emma in the ribs with her elbow. "Just like some good-looking guy around here, eh?"

With a laugh, Aunty Joy twisted away from them,

offering her plate to the couple standing behind them, then moving beyond them to the next cluster of celebrants. Once again, Emma was left frowning with no one but Matt to complain to.

"What is with everyone tonight?" She seemed utterly bewildered. "Where are they getting this idea that you and I are a couple?"

"Maybe because we do everything together?" Matt suggested.

"But we only do the things *friends* do," she insisted.

"Like going to the movies, or out to dinner . . ."

Matt was beginning to sound amused. But Emma wasn't.

"Those are all things I do with my girl friends too," she insisted.

"They are also things men and women do on dates," Matt reminded her.

Emma frowned. "But we aren't," she insisted. "We don't hug and kiss and all that stuff. *That's* what people do on dates. And they do romantic things—stuff like walking on the beach in the moonlight, or having dinner by candlelight." She shot him a triumphant look. "We don't do any of that. Let's face it, Matt, you're not the romantic type. There's just no zing between us."

Matt frowned at her. "I'm not the romantic type?"

"Of course not. You're a computer type, Matt. You're scientific, and practical, and straightforward."

"And that's not good?"

"Of course it's good. It's fine. For my friend. But for a boyfriend, I want someone romantic. Someone who surprises me with little presents, who takes me to special places. Someone who makes me hear bells when we kiss."

"Bells?"

As though responding to the inquiry in his voice, bells suddenly began to ring. Sleigh bells. Santa had arrived.

As the children ran screaming with pleasure toward the chubby bearded man in the red aloha shirt, Emma looked after them longingly, ready to join in their fun. But first she wanted to be sure Matt understood.

"There has to be magic between a boyfriend and girlfriend, Matt. That's all I mean. And what we have is very special, but it's just a friendship. A friendship that means the world to me," she added. "But it's not magic."

As she finished speaking, one of her twin nieces ran up, taking hold of her hand and pulling at it. Emma's sister Malia lived on the mainland now, but she had brought her family home for a Hawaiian Christmas. And her two little girls adored their Aunty Emma.

Emma hastened to complete what she wanted to say. "You know the way Poki looks up at you?" she asked Matt, mentioning the golden retriever that he owned. "That's what I'd like."

"You want a dog?" Matt was thoroughly confused now.

Emma clicked her tongue in irritation. "Of course not. I want a guy who adores me, the way Poki adores you."

"Come on, Aunty Emma," little Carrie cried, clutching her aunt's hand and pulling her toward Santa and his bulging bag.

Laughing, Emma hurried after her. She didn't see that Matt was staring after them, a thoughtful look on his face.

"Bells and magic," he repeated quietly to himself. "And adoration. Sheesh," he muttered. "It sounds like some kind of weird ritual." Matt's fierce frown scared off a young cousin who approached him to show off the action figure he'd received from Santa. The startled look on his cousin's face caused Matt's scowl to worsen before he schooled his features into a more amicable configuration.

Pasting a smile on his face, Matt wandered closer to Santa. Perhaps observing the jolly old man would help him. After all, he had sleigh bells, a magic bag, and legions of kids who adored him. Three out of three of Emma's deepest desires. Maybe something would rub off.

Chapter One

"Will you look at that!"

Statewide Bank in Malino, Hawaii, was a friendly place. As in most small towns, everyone was acquainted, so when a customer called out that Valentine's Day afternoon, all present glanced up to see what was happening.

Emma Lindsey was counting out bills for one of the bank regulars, Ben Takashima from the Japanese lunch shop down the street. Standing at her window, Ben was half-turned, staring toward the entrance and completely ignoring the cash and rolls of coins she'd just finished stacking in front of him. Satisfied with the neat mound of cash, Emma followed the direction of his eyes to the door.

A tall young woman had just entered the bank, a

vase of long-stemmed yellow rosebuds, their edges blushed with pink, held in one of her large brown hands. Luana Young's parents owned the general store in Malino. It was a place where residents could buy anything necessary to small-town life. Mr. Young saw to the hardware, the gardening items, and the kitchen supplies. Mrs. Young supervised the small selection of undergarments, the bolts of fabric, and the sewing supplies. And Luana Young was the closest thing Malino had to a florist. She sold plants at her parents' store, and would arrange and deliver bouquets of flowers or create leis for special occasions.

"Oh!" Emma couldn't help the soft exclamation. Her favorite flowers were roses; and her especial favorites were the yellow ones, with the pink-edged petals. She, and everyone else in the bank, waited impatiently and not a little enviously to discover the identity of the recipient.

Standing just inside the entrance to the bank, Luana scanned her clipboard officiously, knowing she was the center of attention and enjoying every second. A member of a prominent hula *halau*, she was a performer who knew how to hold a moment. Along the line waiting for a teller, people turned to one another, trying to guess the identity of the lucky recipient.

Emma felt a tug of jealousy so deep it shocked her.

"I wonder who the lucky lady is," she said, handing Ben his bank bag, the money for his register still heaped on the counter between them and temporarily forgotten.

Along with everyone else present, Emma was watching Luana to see who would be receiving those beautiful roses. One of the employees, obviously. Even in a town as small as Malino, Luana wouldn't track someone down in the midst of her errands to deliver a vase of flowers, even flowers as exceptional as these.

Emma sighed. They couldn't possibly be for her. Except for Matt—and he didn't really count—she hadn't had a Valentine since the ninth grade. Clement Chong. Acne and glasses, and so shy he could barely form a coherent sentence when he was near her.

That left four other women to chose from. It was a small branch, with only five employees.

As Luana played up her moment, walking slowly forward, letting everyone get a good look at the beautiful long-stemmed roses she had provided, Emma considered the others. Her good friend Kim Asencion hadn't said anything recently that would indicate they might be for her. In fact, just last week she'd complained that she hadn't had a date for over a month.

Emma shifted her focus to Corinne Peralto, the part-time teller. Corinne was a college sophomore and Emma knew she didn't have a regular boyfriend. Corinne was always talking about dates, but she rarely mentioned the same name twice. It seemed doubtful that a one-time date would send such an extravagant bouquet. And could another college student afford such beautiful long-stemmed roses?

Emma, her eyes still following Luana's progress, considered the other two, older, employees. Sandy, the customer service rep, had just gone through an acrimonious divorce. Scratch her.

So it must be for their manager, Nishiko Tanaka. Whoever would have suspected that her serious husband would have such a romantic streak? Hideo worked for one of the large resorts, in some type of financial capacity. Emma had only once seen him without a tie, at the town Christmas party. He'd worn a red aloha shirt then, tucked neatly into his khaki slacks.

Emma shook her head. I guess you just never know, she thought. One thing was certain. Hideo could definitely afford a dozen roses, even at the outrageous prices charged on Valentine's Day.

In a hush of expectancy, Luana approached the tellers, sliding alongside the roped-off line. No one seemed to mind that business was at a standstill. The slap of Luana's rubber slippers against her heels and the hum of the electronic equipment were the only sounds to be heard.

When Luana finally stopped at the window and handed over the flowers, there was a quick sound of approval followed by a swift round of applause from the bystanders.

Emma stood with the heavy vase in her hands, a

look of stunned surprise on her face. She barely broke out of it when Luana pushed the clipboard at her.

"Sign on the bottom line, please."

When Emma continued to stare, Luana repeated herself, adding, "I've got more deliveries today."

"Oh. Of course." Emma snapped out of her trance, setting the vase of roses down at the end of her counter and scribbling her name.

Everyone around her, from Kim at the window to her left to Ben standing in front of her, wanted to know who had sent the flowers. Even Nishiko and Sandy were standing behind their desks, leaning forward, looking over expectantly. And although Luana had claimed other deliveries, she too lingered, her hand on the door. Every customer in the bank strained to see as Emma reached for the card. She fumbled with it, her nervous fingers clumsy with shocked delight. Finally, she managed to slip the card from the tiny envelope. Her voice husky with emotion, she read: "From a secret admirer."

The bank exploded with a loud hum of conversation. Speculation was rife. It was a small town, after all. Everyone knew everyone else, knew who was dating whom. . . .

Emma's cheeks turned a becoming shade of pink.

And everyone knew Emma Lindsey. Emma who hadn't had a serious date since she'd returned home last summer. Emma, who'd rarely had a serious date in the whole of her life in Malino.

So who had sent the beautiful—and expensive—bouquet? And on this most romantic of days.

Although Emma swore that she hadn't a clue as to the identity of the sender, everyone was sure she must know him.

"You think real hard, Emma," advised Aunty Liliuokalani. The old woman, "aunty" to the whole town, had always claimed a special affinity with Emma because they were both named after Hawaiian queens. "You know who it is in your subconscious. Eventually, you'll realize who he is." She nodded wisely.

But Emma was lost. In the whole town, she could think of no one who seemed appropriate as the sender of her beautiful flowers.

"Matt Correa," her next customer declared firmly, as she slapped down her check and her deposit slip.

Emma blinked at her. Camelia Ahuna was the neighbor who lived on the other side of Matt's house. Camelia was a little older than Emma's mother and Matt's, who had been the best of friends. But she'd still been a friend of theirs, so Emma and Matt had known her forever.

"The flowers," she said.

Emma, finally grasping the fact that Camelia was guessing the identity of the secret admirer, smiled. "Oh, I don't think so. He's not the type to send anonymous gifts." She glanced lovingly at the bouquet. "Or something so impractical as cut flowers. He'd be more likely to give me an orchid plant. In person."

Camelia shook her head. She was a reticent woman, and apparently she didn't feel any more discussion was necessary.

Word spread rapidly about the gift and its unknown sender. Friday afternoons were always busy, but that afternoon it was crowded enough to sprout half-serious jokes about a run on the bank. Numerous townspeople stopped in to see Emma's flowers for themselves and to speculate on the sender.

Emma worked in a rose-scented daze. At every stray moment, her eyes caressed the beautiful bouquet. Candy for the eyes, she thought. Perfume for the nose. And if she leaned over just so, the petals brushed lightly across her cheek, softer than any silk scarf. Truly a sensual feast.

Over and over, Matt's name arose as the sender of the roses. Again and again, Emma dismissed the possibility. Why couldn't people accept that a man and a woman could be friends without being involved in a romantic way? Of course, Emma smiled, other names had come up too. Everyone from Ben Takashima, who had been standing in front of her when the flowers arrived, to old Mr. Jardine, the retired policeman who banked with Statewide and was extremely fond of Emma.

When it was finally quitting time, she picked the vase up carefully. With advice from the others, she was able to store it safely in her car for the drive home, the glass vase supported by old beach towels and squashed paper bags. The car smelled so good, she thought she could probably spend the whole weekend just sitting in her room sniffing—and be perfectly happy.

How quickly things change, Emma decided as she pulled out of the bank parking lot. Wasn't it just that morning that she'd moaned about her dull life? Standing outside the bank, drinking in the beautiful morning, dreaming of picnics in the park and moonlight strolls on the beach?

She took a deep breath, inhaling the delicate scent of the flowers, and laughed out loud. It had been nothing more than a momentary fit of depression, she decided now, brought on by memories of too many Valentine disappointments. A quick vision of Clement Chong returned and she smiled. She'd run into his mother at the grocery store in Kamuela two weeks ago and learned he had just received another promotion at the big corporation he worked for in Honolulu. He may have been awkward and shy in high school, but he was making an impact in the business world. Things changed. People changed.

Except for Emma Lindsey.

Despite her happy mood, Emma sighed. All her former classmates seemed to be moving successfully up the career ladder or happily married and having children. Or both. Many of them had left their tiny home town and established new lives on the mainland or in Honolulu. How she wished she was one of them.

She'd already driven past the collection of tired wooden buildings that made up the town of Malino, Hawaii. It didn't take but a moment. Malino meant "quiet" and it was that all right, she thought. There was the bank, the post office, the police station. There was the Young's general store and another one that sold basic necessities like milk and bread and toilet tissue. It was an expensive store, used mainly for last-minute emergencies. Most of the townspeople drove into one of the larger towns several times a month to stock up at the big supermarkets there.

There were a few eating places. Three generations of Takashimas had operated the little Japanese lunch shop that had no real name, just a large faded sign in the window that read "sushi" and "box lunch." There was a seafood restaurant that had changed ownership several times over the past twenty years and was currently owned by a family from Arizona. The name had changed as often as the ownership, but it didn't bother any of the local people. They all referred to it as "the seafood place," just as they always had. And there was the Dairy Queen, a quarter mile from the rest of the town and the local gathering place.

Emma had dreamed of leaving Malino for a glamorous job with a major international company, a job that would entail traveling to charming and exotic locales. Unrealistic, she now thought, but she had seemed so close. During her last semester at the university in Honolulu, she had spoken with recruiters on campus, and one of the mainland companies had expressed interest in bringing her to Seattle for a second interview. It hadn't been a job offer, but she had been assured by others that it was more than promising.

Then, just as she finished her exams, her father collapsed, right in the middle of the Sunday morning service. Even immediate attention from a doctor in the congregation had been unable to save him. Emma had headed home, and home she'd stayed. How could she leave her mother who was in such a state of shock? The job at Statewide where she'd worked summers was offered. How could she refuse? She hadn't even returned to Honolulu to collect her things; her roommates had mailed everything to her instead.

Actually, it hadn't been such a bad year, she thought, as she turned off the main road. Her mother was managing much better these days. Matt had returned to town two years ago and it had been easy to fall back into their pattern of friendship. Things between them were great, just like old times. Their friendship was what carried her through—his friendship and her supply of romantic novels.

Some people went on fabulous trips; some had wonderful courtships and romantic weddings. Some were in traffic accidents! *But nothing ever happens to me*, Emma thought. *My life is dull, dull, dull.* She thanked the publishing houses for her beloved books. Her only excitement these days came through the vicarious experiences of the heroines in her novels.

Until today. No doubt about it, the flowers signaled a change in her life. Her sudden smile caused a passing motorist to flash a *shaka* sign at her. The expression of goodwill warmed her heart. She was almost home. And she couldn't wait to show Matt her flowers and tell him all about her day.

"Oh, Matt, I've had the most exciting day!"

Matt was in the kitchen when Emma exploded into his house, the wide skirt of her red muumuu floating out around her swiftly moving legs. She held the glass vase of roses carefully before her, her attention more on it than on Matt or where she was going. Poki, Matt's golden retriever, rushed to meet her and caught her mood. He danced with joy around her.

As she moved across the room, expertly avoiding the exuberant dog, Emma's dark, shoulder-length hair floated out around her head like a mass of *limu* in the sea. However, unlike seaweed, which clung mainly to rocks, her hair curled finely around the fragile white petals of the three small gardenias nestled into the dark mass just above her right ear.

As Emma set the vase of fragrant blossoms on the end of the counter, Matt reached out, brushing some of the fine strands away from her face. His fingers brushed gently against her cheek, and Emma smiled at him.

"Thanks, Matt. You're such a dear." Her full attention still on her flowers, Emma barely glanced at him. "Wait till you hear what happened!"

Too excited to be still, Emma stepped away as she began to tell him about receiving the wonderful gift. Matt returned to filling the coffeemaker, watching her as she spoke. She was an animated speaker, waving her hands to illustrate points as she talked. She barely stopped for a breath, and she spoke quickly, anxious to tell her old friend everything that had happened that day. Poki trotted beside her, watching her hands carefully, his body tense with repressed excitement. Sometimes she threw a tennis ball for him with just such arm movements.

But Poki was to be disappointed. Emma's mind was far from tennis balls and doggie games this evening.

"It was right after lunch and there were all these people in the bank," she told Matt. One arm barely missed the handle of the refrigerator as she flung it wide to indicate the number of customers waiting in line. "And Luana came in—with this absolutely gorgeous bouquet of roses." Her other hand flew out toward the vase she'd placed so carefully on the counter, her fingertips stopping just short of the partially opened petals. "And the whole bank suddenly grew quiet, everybody watching to see who would get them."

Emma twirled back toward Matt and caught the tolerant gaze he had turned on her. He probably thought she was behaving like a four-year-old on Christmas morning. Or perhaps he was just smiling in disbelief at her story.

"It's true. You could have heard a pin drop."

"I believe you," he assured her.

"And Matt—oh, I can still hardly believe it—they were for me!"

"I figured." He grinned.

Emma laughed. "I guess that part was obvious, huh?"

"Unless you stole them from Kim or Nishiko, and I don't think either of them would have let you get away with that."

Matt walked over for a better look at the bouquet. "So who are they from?"

For the first time since she'd entered the room Emma's face lost its cheerful good humor. While still happy, she managed to look miserable at the same time—a strange combination. Her recently animated hands now lay quietly at her sides. Poki, sensing the change in mood, tucked his nose into her hand to lend comfort.

"I don't know who sent them."

Before Matt could ask, Emma held up her hands, palms outward. "I know what you're going to say. Yes, there was a card, but it said 'from a secret admirer'."

Matt let out a low whistle. "Pretty exciting, I'd say. Romantic even." He reached out to pet Poki, who had come to his side, tail wagging, apparently in response to the whistle.

"Oh, I know," Emma agreed, the last word a long breathy sigh. "It's *really* romantic." Emma clasped her hands to her heart, a theatrical gesture that nevertheless managed to look natural when she did it. "I'm so wired I can hardly stay still. And I couldn't *wait* to tell you, but then I was afraid to leave the house in case he called. But Mom said she'd holler over if I have a phone call. From him, I mean." She scrunched up her nose. "So far all the calls have been from people who want to know if he's called yet. How can he call if they're tying up the phone?" Her voice ended in a melodramatic wail.

"Well, there's call waiting. Very handy in these circumstances. You have call waiting, don't you?"

Emma glared at him. Men! Here she was having a crisis of immense proportions, and all he could think about was call waiting!

"That's not the point," she began. Then she decided against debating the issue. He wouldn't understand anyway. As he proved by his next statement.

"I was hoping you'd walk over to the Dairy Queen with me for burgers and sundaes. I haven't given you your valentine." Poki heard the word "walk" and his tail began to wag. Matt patted him absently. "But I guess you won't want to leave the house now."

So maybe he did understand. Emma looked honestly regretful that she had to turn him down. "I would have liked that, Matt. Really, I would. But now . . . Well, I really think I'd better hang around the house tonight. And tomorrow too, maybe. Until he calls, anyway."

Emma moved closer to her roses and took a deep breath. The scent really was too glorious.

"Why don't you come over for dinner? Mom's made chicken stew, and she was just mixing up some biscuits when I left."

Emma stopped pacing and threw herself down on one of the kitchen chairs. The chair objected to the suddenness of her weight with a squeal of protest from legs that pushed a few inches across the linoleum. Poki let out a yelp.

"Sorry, Poki," Emma said. She reached out and scratched behind his ears, earning her a sloppy kiss and an adoring look.

Matt stared at the two of them for a moment before he replied to her dinner invitation.

"Chicken stew sounds good. Shall I bring the coffee? I have some new beans I'm trying out." Matt nodded toward the coffeemaker where the pot was almost full. He maintained a web page for friends with a coffee farm, and he was always sampling beans. They had been trying out plants from different parts of the world, hoping to find something truly different. "These are from Paraguay."

Emma nodded absently, but she barely heard Matt's question or his comment. Her hand remained on Poki's head, absently smoothing the soft fur, but she was in another world. Her brow furrowed briefly as she considered the sender of her flowers.

"Doesn't it seem to you that he might call—for a date or something? Tonight?"

Her hand stilled on Poki's head, then fell into her lap. She turned to face Matt, looking deep into his dark eyes. "You're a guy. If you sent a girl a dozen long-stemmed roses for Valentine's Day wouldn't you call that night and ask for a date?"

Emma stared at Matt for a short moment, then shook her head before he even had a chance to answer.

"No, never mind. You'd never do that, anyway."

She rose from her chair and started across the room toward her vase of roses. Poki padded along behind her. "Bring your valentine," she called over her shoulder. "And the coffee too. Mom made some heart-shaped cookies for dessert." She picked up the vase, took a deep breath of the delicious fragrance, and started toward the door.

But Matt's voice called her back.

"Wait a minute. What do you mean I'd never do that? Why wouldn't I send a woman a dozen roses?"

Emma returned the vase to the counter and faced Matt. She was surprised to see that he seemed upset. "Oh, Matt, I didn't mean to offend you. It's just that you're not the type to send a dozen long-stemmed roses. You're the kind of guy who would take over an orchid plant and hand it to your girl. Then you'd tell her what kind of light it needed, and how to water and fertilize it." She shrugged. "Nothing wrong with that. It's just . . ." She paused. ". . . different," she finished with triumph. Yes, different. It was the perfect word. Not better, not worse, just different.

"Not too romantic," Matt admitted.

"No," Emma agreed, "but not bad either. You're just a different kind of person than the guy who chose these flowers."

Emma flew across the kitchen and placed a quick kiss on his cheek. "But that's okay, 'cause I love you anyway, Matt."

She patted his arm, then went back for her vase.

"Come on over. Dinner should be ready any time." She smiled. "Oh, it would be nice if you brought some of that great coffee of yours."

And she was gone.

Frowning after her, Matt reached for the coffeepot. He pulled a thick pot-holder from a hook beside the stove, using it to support the bottom of the hot pot. Poki followed along, looking up at Matt with great sad eyes when he was ordered back inside.

Chapter Two

Emma greeted Matt with a sad smile.

"Still no call."

She sat at the kitchen table, at the end closest to the wall phone. If it rang, she could pick up the receiver with just a twist of her body and a reaching of her arm, without leaving her seat. The vase of roses sat in all their glory in the center of the worn table, filling the room with their delicate fragrance. She had found one of the hand-crocheted doilies made by her late grandmother and placed it beneath the vase.

Sonia Lindsey was standing at the sink, washing biscuit dough from her hands. A pan of baking powder biscuits sat on the counter, ready for the oven.

"Hi, Matt. How you doing? Did you see Emma's

roses?" She smiled at him as she wiped her hands on an embroidered cotton towel, and winked at him.

Emma turned her head quickly toward Matt. She could have sworn her mother *winked* at him. What could her mother be thinking?

"Hi, Mrs. Lindsey." Matt offered a wry grin, raising the coffeepot he held, inquiring with a look about where he should put it. Sonia gestured to the stove, so Matt placed the pot on an empty burner and set it on warm. Then he stole a heart-shaped cookie from the platter on the counter and joined Emma at the table.

"No call while you were gone, huh?"

Emma sighed. "No." She shifted in the chair and leaned forward, resting her elbows on the table and plopping her head on her hands. "I just don't understand it."

Matt raised his hands to show her the envelope he held. "I brought your valentine."

Emma tried to smile. Matt's voice was light and teasing and she knew he was trying to cheer her. They had been neighbors forever, it seemed, and they had exchanged Valentine cards since preschool. As they grew older their friends became certain they were a couple, but Emma and Matt always claimed to be nothing more than good friends.

"I can't *date* Matt," Emma told her girlfriends. "He's my best friend in the world. Dating him would just ruin our friendship."

Holding the red envelope in her hand, brooding over

the now silent telephone, Emma heard her mother click her tongue.

Sonia squeezed Matt's shoulder affectionately as she walked by him on her way from the oven. "You probably sent them, huh, and she's waiting around for some stranger to call."

Emma looked over at Matt curiously, still clutching the envelope in her hand. Matt? How could her mother think it was Matt? Those people at the bank were different. They didn't know her and Matt the way she did. The way her mother did. Sonia should know better. Matt was her old dear friend. She would never chance losing his friendship by getting into a romantic relationship with him. Nothing could kill a friendship faster than starting to date. Ask anyone who dated a business associate.

Besides, Matt was too practical to send her a dozen roses.

"Me? Why would you think it was me? You know, I got at least a dozen calls this afternoon asking if I sent Emma some yellow roses."

Emma's eyes widened. "A dozen calls?" She swatted his arm with her hand. "And you pretended to be so surprised while I went on and on telling you all about it!"

Matt offered a sheepish smile. "You were having so much fun telling me. I didn't want to spoil it for you."

Dear old Matt.

"Besides," Matt continued, "I wouldn't have sent roses. Waste of money, cut flowers."

"Exactly what I was just thinking," Emma declared.

"I would have given Emma an orchid plant," Matt went on. "Handed it right over to her, and told her what kind of light it needed, and how to water it . . ."

He stopped with a laugh when Emma attacked him with a dish towel. "Oh, you! Think you're funny, do you?"

Sonia watched them with an indulgent expression, not sure what they were laughing about, but happy to hear it. She watched him fight off the flying towel for a minute, then stopped it by asking them to set the table.

Matt stood immediately to help, but Emma returned to her chair, claiming the need to open her valentine first. Sonia scolded, but Matt shrugged it off.

"That's okay. I'll get the plates while Emma reads the card."

Grateful, Emma smiled at him and tore at the red envelope.

"I feel just terrible, because I was going to buy yours after work. I thought it would be fun reading through all the cards on Valentine's Day, you know, and choosing that special one. But I was so excited about the roses, I just plain forgot."

She opened the large card carefully, smiling with pleasure as she read the message. Matt always knew just what to get for her. It was a shame that he was such an old and valued friend because he was going to make some woman an awfully nice husband someday.

But that woman would not be Emma Lindsey. Emma wanted someone mysterious, someone she didn't know like a member of her own family. Someone romantic, who always knew what the situation called for and what his special woman needed. Someone like the hero in her latest romantic novel. Someone who would create fireworks for her, make her hear bells when they kissed.

Someone like the mysterious gentleman who had surprised her with a dozen pink-tipped yellow roses.

She blinked back her wandering thoughts and reread the card.

"It's a wonderful card, Matt," she told him, jumping up and giving him a swift kiss. "I feel just awful about not getting yours."

"Don't worry about it. I understand."

Matt's arm closed around her and he held her tight alongside his body for a moment. A light squeeze let her know he didn't hold it against her that she had forgotten his card. Which only made her feel worse. And probably explained the strange warm tingle that traveled up her spine. A tickly sensation, it started in the small of her back, at the base of her spine, just below her waist, and worked its way up to her neck, causing the little hairs there to prickle, and making her squirm in Matt's grasp.

The oven timer went off and Matt released her. Emma shivered again, feeling suddenly cold without his warm arm around her. She moved instinctively toward the oven, open and spewing heat as Sonia removed the pan of evenly browned biscuits.

When she realized what she was doing, she detoured toward the cupboard and removed three cups. She filled them from Matt's coffeepot and set them onto saucers at each place just as Sonia put the stew pot in the center of the table—right in the spot where her roses had been. Emma's head flew around, searching the room for her bouquet.

"Now, don't worry about your flowers," Sonia told her. "They'll be just fine on the counter there while we eat."

Emma turned her eyes toward the counter beside the back door. Her bouquet sat there in all its glory, sending its sweet fragrance across the room. Even with the delicious scents of chicken, gravy, and biscuits, Emma could still smell her beautiful roses.

She sat down facing the bouquet, with a huge smile on her face and both dimples showing. The momentary pang she'd felt was completely forgotten. What a great Valentine's Day this was!

Two days later, Emma pulled the sleeves of her oversize sweater down over her wrists as she sat in the old wooden chair. Poki sat beside her, his head in her lap, his large brown eyes oozing sympathy. Emma was sure he didn't know why she was so sad, but he was willing to be sad with her.

The sun was going down on a beautiful Sunday evening, flaming the western sky with orange and pink. But with it went the comfortable warmth of the day. Emma felt cold and welcomed the heat Poki was so willing to share.

As she stroked the dog's golden head, she looked around Matt's lanai, at the potted crotons and the brightly painted Adirondack chairs. Matt had made the chairs with his Dad one summer many years ago, and Emma had helped them paint each one a different color. Red, yellow, orange, purple, green, and blue. The colorful chairs had quickly become Matt and Emma's favorite place to sit and talk.

With the sensitivity they'd always seemed to have for each other, Matt approached the chair with two mugs of steaming coffee. Emma had her hands wrapped gratefully around her mug before he'd even had a chance to sit. She took a deep sniff.

"Mmm, thanks," she said. "I love the smell of coffee."

"So do I," Matt agreed.

Emma took another deep breath. "Ohh, did you put chocolate in it?"

"Yep. No taste testing tonight. I thought you could use a little treat."

Emma smiled. “You spoil me, Matt.”

He shrugged, took a sip, then balanced the mug on the arm of the chair. “So, was there a call? From the secret admirer?”

Emma shook her head. He knew she would have run over immediately to tell him about such a call. He was just asking so she could talk about it. Her friend Matt, the shrink.

“No. I don’t get it. I was so sure . . .” She sipped tentatively at the hot liquid, keeping both hands firmly around the warm mug. “I’ve spent all weekend inhaling the heady perfume of my roses . . .”

“And reading romance novels.”

“How did you know?” Emma grinned at Matt over the edge of her mug, showing one sassy dimple.

He had to grin back. “Aw, come on. The heady perfume of your roses?” Disgust at the pretty phrasing laced his words.

It felt good to laugh, Emma decided. She’d spent too long cooped up in the house waiting for a phone call that hadn’t materialized. She’d even canceled her regular Saturday morning tennis game with Matt because there was no call on Friday night. She had been so sure it would come yesterday morning. But the numerous phone calls she did receive had all been from friends asking for updates.

Emma smiled over at Matt. “I knew coming over here was the right thing to do. You always make me feel better.”

Matt watched Emma carefully. "Did it occur to you that he might plan to send another gift before he makes himself known?"

Emma's eyes widened as she sat bolt upright, almost sending a rush of hot coffee into Matt's lap. The sudden movement spooked Poki, too, who jumped back with a yelp, startled. "Oh. I never thought of that. Wouldn't that be exciting?!"

Matt sent her a wry smile. "And you call yourself a romantic?"

Emma was suddenly too excited to hold onto her mug. She set it down on the table beside the chair and jumped up. Poki took a quick sniff of the mug then scurried after her. For several minutes she paced up and down beside him while Matt watched, sipping his coffee. Poki followed along, his step eager. Although she was silent, her arms swung out around her the way they did when she talked and her facial expressions changed with her jumping thoughts.

Finally Emma fell back into place beside him. She reached over for her cup and took a healthy gulp. "I like it. It's just the kind of thing someone like him would do."

"Someone like him?"

"Of course. A true romantic."

She turned to face Matt. "I can't believe I didn't think of it. Thanks, Matt. You know, there might be hope for you after all." She leaned over the wide wooden chair arms and kissed his cheek.

"I can't wait to tell Mom."

She handed him her empty mug, then headed off across the lawn.

Emma and Matt sat over their usual after-dinner coffee the following night, Emma babbling in her usual animated style, her eyes sparkling, her dimples flashing intermittently.

Emma was no longer mooning over the lack of a phone call. She had had another exciting day at work.

"So I think I know who the secret admirer is," Emma said. "I talked with Kim earlier and with Mom over dinner, and they agree it might be him."

She paused to take a sip, running the tip of her tongue over her upper lip afterward. As she looked up afterward, Emma caught a strange look on Matt's face.

"What's the matter?"

Matt blinked at her, as though pulling his thoughts back from far away.

"Nothing. Ah, just reviewing a new game idea. Sorry." He reached down to scratch Poki's head. "Go on. So you know who the secret admirer is?"

"Well, I don't *know*." Emma wiggled in her chair, her temporary ire at Matt's distraction gone. "You see there's this customer who comes in almost every day. He brings in the money from that restaurant—the seafood one down the street?"

Matt looked up, nodding to indicate that he knew the one she meant and she rushed on.

"Well, he always flirts a little, you know? But today he was asking about the roses."

Emma laughed and Matt smiled in response.

"It seems everyone has heard about the roses. It's such fun. Everyone who came in today mentioned it, whether they were at my window or not. The only time I've seen anything like this at the bank was when Sandy had her baby. Everybody wanted to know all about it."

"Well, this was definitely the easier way to accomplish it."

Emma looked puzzled. "Accomplish what?"

Then it dawned on her what he meant and she blushed. "Oh . . . Yeah, I'd take this over having a baby any day."

Her eyes softened. "Of course, one day I would like a baby. Someday when I'm married and all. Sandy's baby is such a cute little thing."

She finished her coffee and put the mug on the table. No use thinking about that now. No matter how much she wanted a child, she couldn't have a family until she found someone to share her life with. And while she now had a promising prospect, he still hadn't called! But her life was a lot more exciting than it had been.

"Having everyone talking about my flowers is a lot of fun. You know, some of them even went over to the store to talk to Luana and her mother, trying to find out who sent them. But they claim they don't know." Emma pushed a strand of hair out of her eyes and sighed. "I hadn't even thought of calling them. Luana told Kim that someone left the money and instructions on what they wanted in an envelope at the store. And that's all she knows."

"But you think this restaurant guy is the one?"

Emma tucked one foot under her on the wide chair. Poki, lounging on the floor between them with his head on his paws, looked up at the movement. "Oh, yes, I do. He just kept asking about the roses, and teasing me about my guy. And what would he think of next. That's the part that convinced me—the 'what's next.' It's just like you said, that he must be waiting to send another surprise. It seems like it has to be him, don't you think?"

"Mmm." Matt considered. "Could be. Did he ask you out?"

"Nooo." Her grin grew with the length of the vowel. "But he did make a big point about seeing me tomorrow. You know, when he brings in the deposit. So maybe then . . ."

Matt put his mug down beside his chair. "You seem to be enjoying this."

"Oh, I am. I can't tell you how much."

"You don't have to tell me. I can see it."

His voice was soft, intimate. Emma smiled over at

him before leaning forward to bestow a soft kiss on his cheek.

"You're such a great friend, Matt. It wouldn't be half as much fun if I couldn't talk it over with you over coffee every evening."

The next day, Emma arrived early at Matt's back door. She was so anxious to talk to Matt, she'd come over before cleaning up the dinner dishes. Because she was early, he wasn't out on the lanai waiting for her and she had to knock at the kitchen door. Poki responded with loud barking.

Matt opened the door. "Emma. Come inside. It's cold tonight; we might as well sit in the kitchen."

Poki immediately changed from guard dog mode to devoted friend. He pranced excitedly around Emma's feet, tail wagging. Emma patted him, barely noticing the automatic gesture.

"Oh, dear. I interrupted your dinner." Emma sniffed deeply. "Mmmm, that smells wonderful. Your cooking must be getting better."

Matt laughed. "Well, thanks, I think. But much as I appreciate the compliment, I can't accept it. It's Stouffer's." He sat down before a half-finished plate of lasagna and Poki took up his usual place beside his master's chair. The dog's eyes followed each forkful from plate to mouth.

Emma shrugged. "Doesn't matter. Smells terrific.

I'd definitely eat it myself. They make great stuff for the microwave these days."

Emma checked the coffeemaker, determined that the coffee was ready, and poured herself a cup.

"So what brings you rushing over here tonight? More news in the bouquet of roses soap opera?"

Emma frowned. "Soap opera? Gee, Matt, I don't know if I like that comparison." She pursed her lips in consideration. "Mom watches a couple of soap operas, you know. And the story lines can get pretty weird."

"Okay. My mom watched them too." He considered for a moment. "How about the romance of your roses?"

"I like that." She sipped at her coffee, determined that it was not tongue-searing hot, and took another longer drink. "The Romance of the Roses. I definitely like it."

"Sounds like the title of one of your books." Matt's voice was even but hardly enthusiastic.

Emma smiled at Matt. She knew he wanted to hear the latest developments and she couldn't resist teasing him a little. He'd finished his dinner, so she picked up his plate and carried it to the sink, bringing another mug of coffee on her way back. Poki, disappointed at seeing the plate disappear, lay down beside Matt's chair.

Emma took her time seating herself, sneaking a peek at Matt. He was watching her, a small smile playing at the corners of his mouth. She knew that look. He knew she was teasing and he'd wait all night before he'd ask again. She didn't have the patience to outwait him and he knew it. She laughed in resignation. Matt gave her a satisfied smile.

"Remember that guy I told you about yesterday? The one who works at the seafood place?"

"Sure. Did he admit that he's your secret admirer?"

"Oh, no. I think he's playing it out for all it's worth. He waited for me to be free today, though." Emma wiggled back into the chair, too agitated to sit calmly. "He could have gone to Kim's window, but he waited for mine to be free. And he was flirting again."

It was always hard for Emma to stay seated when she was excited. Now she got up and paced around the table. Poki got to his feet and followed. "Oh, Matt, I can hardly stand it. We're going out for dinner tomorrow."

Matt's smile wavered, but Emma didn't notice. Poki, however, stopped pacing with Emma and sat beside Matt's chair. He rested his head in his master's lap and turned large sad eyes up to him.

Emma continued to rattle on about her upcoming date. "I can hardly wait. What do you think he'll do?"

"He'd better not *do* anything," Matt declared, his lips set in a tight line.

Emma dismissed him with a wave. "Honestly, Matt. Don't be silly. Sometimes you act like my father."

Mention of her father stilled her pacing for an instant. Her eyes clouded, filled with unshed tears. Matt's sympathetic smile made her feel better. She knew he understood. After all, he'd lost his father unexpectedly too. She smiled, a quivery but brave effort.

Then she blinked and resumed her journey around the kitchen table.

But Matt wasn't done with this topic yet.

"Someone has to watch out for you."

His voice, soft and caring, reached out to her, and seemed to envelop her. She sat.

"Thank you, Matt." She smiled at him across the table, tried a sip of her cooled coffee, wrinkled up her nose at it, then attempted to spear him with a stern gaze. "But you don't have to act like a tough big brother all the time."

Matt grinned. "Okay. How about if I do it just long enough to let your dates know there's someone looking out for you?"

Emma took a paper napkin from the plastic holder on the table, wadded it up, and threw it at him. Sensing a game, Poki gave a short bark then stood beside Matt, tail wagging, alert and impatient to be part of the action.

But within a minute, Emma was back to pacing, speculating about the possible activities her romantic admirer might provide. Poki trailed along behind her, ready for further games. But Emma was far away in a land of her imagining, thinking about what might occur the following evening. Candlelight dinners, moonlight picnics, starlit rides in *paniolo* country, all seemed possibilities for someone romantic enough to surprise her with roses on Valentine's Day.

Matt listened quietly as he refilled her mug, his expression closed and somber. When he voiced his doubts, she waved them away. She didn't expect Matt to understand.

"Don't be silly, Matt. Anyone who could plan such a delicious surprise—and expensive too—has got to have something else wonderful hidden up his sleeve."

She slipped back into her chair and picked up her mug. Surprised by the steaming hot liquid it held, she put it down and bounced up again, heading for the door. Poki followed.

"I'd better go home and check the closet. He's picking me up at work so I'll have to chose something that I can wear both to dinner and the bank."

She rushed back across the room to plant a kiss on Matt's cheek, surprising Poki who raced back after her. But she ignored the dog, sprinting straight out the door on her important mission. She left Poki restive, running between Matt and the closed door.

Matt watched the dog's futile chase. "I know just how you feel, boy." He shook his head. "You thought she was going to play with you. But you just never know what a woman's going to do."

Matt got up and reached for his jacket. "Come on. I'll take you for a walk. We guys have to stick together."

Chapter Three

At first, Matt thought he'd imagined the knock at his door. But Poki, sleeping on the floor at his feet, jumped up instantly, running toward the kitchen and barking loudly. A cold wind whipped around the house, causing creaks and groans. Without Poki's keen ears, Matt would have thought it was just another outside noise. With a swift glance at the clock, he followed Poki through the house. A quick peek outside and he threw open the door.

A disheveled Emma blew in with the cold night air. She was inadequately dressed for the chilly evening, shivering and gripping her sweater tightly about her. Matt reacted instinctively, wrapping her in his arms to share his own body heat. Poki leapt around them, delighted with this unexpected guest.

For an indeterminable period of time, they stood together, right there in the kitchen, in front of the back door, Emma enfolded in Matt's arms. No words were spoken. None were needed. Matt recognized a need in his dear friend and filled it. Poki, with his instinctive canine understanding, stood quietly beside them, his head nudging at Emma's hand.

Matt held Emma for what seemed like hours. For what seemed only a second. His body was warm and comfortable. Familiar. She was safe now.

Finally she shivered—a long, deep shudder that shook her whole body—and pushed away from him.

"Thank you, Matt. I needed that." She leaned down. "And thank you, Poki," she added. She rubbed her hand over the dog's head, still snuggled against her.

Matt led her to the door at the opposite end of the room and pushed her toward his den. When he'd returned home after his parents were lost at sea in a boating accident, he'd remade the living room into a home office and christened it his den. The longest wall was covered with bookshelves; his large desk, with the latest in computer equipment, sat beneath the window. There was a sofa and a recliner and a wooden rocking chair of his mother's that seemed woefully out of place. There was also a television that he rarely watched, and a stereo that he listened to constantly. Keali'i Reichel's voice filled the room when they entered, singing a love song with Lorna Lim.

"What you need is a cup of hot chocolate," Matt

told Emma, pointing her toward the sofa. "You go on in and sit down. I'll join you in a minute." He looked at Poki. "You go too and keep her company."

Poki obediently followed Emma, who dragged her feet over to the sofa, settling into the corner against one heavily upholstered arm. Matt returned quickly, placing a mug of hot chocolate into her hands.

As he handed her the mug, Matt looked at Emma's long legs. Emma had lovely legs, and like any male, he enjoyed looking at them. But tonight they were encased in nothing heavier than panty hose. And an awful lot of them showed. Listening to the wind whipping around the house, he realized why she was so cold. A cute little pleated skirt was all he could see of her outfit beneath the long sweater, little being the operative word. Even her sweater was not particularly heavy, being made of cotton rather than wool, which might have offered more warmth. Hawaii might be a tropical paradise, but it did get cold in February. Mauna Kea had been covered with snow that morning, and with the cold and rain they were having now, there would probably be even more snow tonight. The *mauka* winds blowing across that snow cover brought cold air to the rest of the island.

With a quick movement, Matt reached beneath the end table for the old afghan kept there. He spread it over Emma's lap and tucked it around her legs.

"There." He smiled with satisfaction. "That should help."

"Thanks." Emma smiled gently, still sipping at her chocolate. What would she do without Matt?

Her eyes drifted to Poki, sitting on the floor beside her, his head on her knee, his adoring eyes lifted to her face. What she'd give to see that look in a man's eyes!

She could feel Matt watching her as she sipped the chocolate. Warm eyes, full of questions. He'd be wondering what she was doing here . . .

No, he probably wasn't. He'd be imagining all kinds of things that might have happened. They'd always been in tune that way. It really was too bad there was no magic between them. She loved Matt, just not as a boyfriend. Theirs was a platonic friendship. He was the brother she'd never had. Though there was a moment there, when he'd held her in his arms . . .

She shook her head. No, that was silly. Of course she'd felt his warmth enter her body, warming her from the inside out. That was what he'd meant to do. Because he could see how cold she was. It was the friendly thing to do. A brother would have done the same.

And that little shiver—okay, that big shiver. That was just her body's reaction to the shift from warmth back to cold when he released her. The blood she'd felt rushing though her veins was just her body's way of restoring her normal body temperature. It had nothing to do with Matt.

She sipped again from the mug of chocolate, enjoying the hot liquid sliding down her throat, wrapping both hands around the mug to capture more of its warmth. She was returning to life now, here in the comfortable familiarity of Matt's den, with his mother's old afghan wrapped around her legs and Poki's warm bulk resting against her. Israel Kamakawiwo'ole crooned on the stereo now, his sweet familiar voice helping her relax. The aroma of chocolate from her cup blended with the familiar smell of the room—that indefinable scent of books, of upholstered furniture, of dust even. She sneezed.

"Bless you."

Matt pulled a box of tissues from somewhere and offered it to her just as she sneezed for a second time.

"Bless you again."

"Oh, dear. I hope I didn't catch a cold."

Matt, settling into his reclining chair, shook his head.

"You don't catch colds from being out in the cold. You . . ."

". . . catch colds from germs," she finished with him.

They both laughed. The book he'd been reading when the knock sounded fell to the floor from the arm of the chair where he'd set it aside.

"Oh, no. Now you've lost your place."

"It's okay." Matt watched her as she pulled at the tissue still in her hand. "I'll find it."

Emma tossed the tissue aside and picked up her

mug again, staring down into the rich liquid. She'd rather let her mind drift back to Matt's poor housekeeping skills than to a recounting of her dreadful evening.

Matt cleared his throat and Emma looked up.

"So . . ." he prompted.

She'd have to say something. She could tell he was worried about her. It wasn't like her to be so quiet for so long. Or to remain so still.

"It's not him."

Her voice was flat. The sentence might sound ambiguous or unintelligible to some; but she knew Matt would understand. If Emma had been the type to cry, she would have been sobbing on Matt's shoulder. But since she never cried—well, rarely cried—she sipped her chocolate and began to talk.

"Lance met me at work just like we'd agreed." She gave Matt a crooked smile, just a little one, but enough to reveal a flash of dimple. "Did I ever tell you his name is Lance? Sounds like a character from one of my novels, doesn't it?"

Matt agreed that it did. But she could see that he counted it as just one more mark against the other man.

"Anyway, Lance met me at work. He was very complimentary about how I looked and everything. He gave me a pink carnation. I was sure it was him."

She looked up at Matt with a wry smile. "One carnation isn't much like a dozen roses, but, still, it was a very romantic gesture." Then she shrugged. "But it was downhill from there. We ate at his restaurant—the one where he works, I mean. He gets a discount. And on every table was a little vase with a pink carnation in it." Emma shook her head. "Right then, I knew it couldn't be him. No one would spend a fortune on long-stem roses and then try to save a few bucks on dinner the following week."

Emma set aside the now empty mug and huddled into her corner of the sofa. It was wonderfully warm in the room but she still felt cold inside. Poki nudged his head a little further into her lap and she slid her leg closer to his warm fur.

"Afterward, all we did was stroll around town. That could have been romantic, I guess, if the moon had been full and the air balmy. But it was just too dark and cold tonight. There was no moon, not even any stars." She sighed. "And it rained a little on and off."

Emma wanted to give Lance points for *trying* to be romantic, but it was a strain.

"Lance is a musician." Emma stared hard at the afghan in her lap, picking at a thread that protruded from the crocheted edge. "Apparently restaurant work is a temporary stop gap, so he can eat. All he talked about while we walked was his band and how hard it is to get a good gig."

Emma finally raised her eyes and looked Matt full in the face. "I froze my little you-know-what off. Lance however, must be basically hot-blooded, because he didn't notice the cold at all. I finally told him I had to get home for an important phone call."

Matt came around beside her, resting against the arm of the sofa and pushing her forward to rub her shoulder blades. "Poor little Emma. You've had a very difficult day, haven't you?"

"Mmmm." Emma leaned back into his hands. "That feels so good."

"You're all tensed up. You need to relax."

"That's what I'm doing right now, aren't I?" She smiled up at him, her eyelids half closed. "Lance really isn't such a bad guy. If I didn't have my secret admirer to dream over, and the weather had been better, I might even have enjoyed his company."

Matt leaned over her, so that she could see his skeptical look. She laughed.

"Okay. He still would be boring."

She relaxed back into his hands once more.

"Mmm, you're such a sweetheart to be doing this."

"Well, don't get too used to it." Matt finished with a pat on her head and returned to his chair. "And I'll be expecting like treatment one of these days of course."

Emma scrunched her nose at him, but she was smiling.

"So you're right back where you started."

"Yes. Discouraging, isn't it?" She heaved a giant sigh. It was such a cliché, but it did feel good.

"You still have the fun of guessing who it might

be," Matt suggested. "They do say that anticipation is ninety percent of the fun."

Emma frowned. "Who is 'they' anyway?"

She settled back into the cushions, looking truly relaxed for the first time since they'd entered the room.

"It *is* fun talking to everyone about my secret admirer and debating the possibilities," she admitted. "Even Nishiko got involved."

Emma was beginning to look more like her old self. Especially when she grinned at him, busily massaging Poki's head as she talked.

"You know, even Kim suggested it might be you."

"Me?" Matt's grin was slightly incredulous.

Emma laughed. "I told her she didn't know you at all if she thought you'd spend fifty dollars on a vase of flowers."

Matt frowned at her. "How do you know what it cost?"

"Oh, word has gotten around. Didn't I tell you? Someone left an envelope for Luana, just lying there on the counter in the store. There was a fifty-dollar bill in it and instructions on what to send, who to send it to, and where and all of that." Emma's eyes sparkled with excitement. "Isn't it the most amazing thing you ever heard?"

"Oh, yes." His voice was dry. "Amazing."

Emma laughed. "Well, I find it exciting and amazing and romantic." She threw off the afghan and rose from the sofa, dislodging Poki from his comfortable position beside her. "Thanks for the chocolate and the comfort, Matt."

With quick, efficient movements, she folded the afghan and pushed it back beneath the end table, then headed for the door.

She blew a kiss into her hand and threw it in his direction. It was a game they'd played as children, something each had played with their parents. Matt reached up and caught her kiss, holding it to his heart. Then he threw one in his turn. She dashed out the door still holding his kiss to her heart.

Chapter Four

"Emmy!"

Emma had barely managed to pick up the ringing telephone and say hello when her sister's voice squealed into her ear. She held the receiver away for an instant, frowning at the diminutive of her name that she hated.

"Emma, please, Malia. After all, I don't call you Elaine. The least you could do is return the favor." Malia had been named Elaine Malia after their two grandmothers, and she'd always disliked her first name, preferring since early childhood to be called Malia. No one else in her class was named Elaine, and she'd longed for a "normal" name like Courtney or Kanani. Finally, she'd asked everyone to call her Malia, and she had been E. Malia ever since.

"Sure, Emmy, I mean Emma. It's just that I always think of you as my baby sister, and the Emmy just pops out."

Emma sighed. "You're not *that* much older than I am."

Though that four-year difference in their ages had made quite a difference over the years. For instance, Malia had already finished high school when Emma started. And by the time Emma left for college, Malia had finished nursing school, gotten a job, and met and married Air Force Lieutenant Ron Silva.

Now, Emma had a bachelor's degree in business, and was at home with their mother, trying to ease her through widowhood, and Malia was living in Texas with her husband and their toddlers, twin girls named Carrie and Courtney. They'd been back to visit at Christmas time and Emma dearly missed her two nieces.

"I may not be that much older in years," Malia agreed, "but I can still remember when Mom brought you home from the hospital. And I always called you 'Emmy'," she added.

"Well, please don't any more," Emma requested again. "After all, I'm named for the queen of King Kamehameha the Fourth. You should show a little respect." A laugh rumbled deep in her throat as she reminded her sister of the origin of her name. Their mother had been in Honolulu and visited the Queen Emma Summer Palace while she was pregnant with her second child. She'd been so impressed, she'd determined to name her baby Emma after the queen, if it was a girl. As it had been.

Malia laughed. They had both heard the story of Queen Emma innumerable times from their mother. "Okay, okay. *Emma*," she said, repeating the name very carefully and with emphasis, "I want to hear all about your secret admirer. Have you found out yet who it is?"

Suitably distracted from the topic of names, Emma launched into the story of Lance Kobayashi and their pitiful date. Malia commiserated with her for a while, then Emma told her about her friends' speculation on who her secret admirer might be.

"I can't believe how many people think it's Matt."

"Matt Correa? From next door?"

"Of course. Silly, isn't it?"

Emma was surprised that Malia remained silent for a moment, that she didn't chime in immediately to say how ridiculous that idea was.

"Well?" she persisted. "Isn't that the strangest idea you ever heard?"

"Well, of course I don't know Matt as well as you do," Malia said slowly. "I mostly remember him as a little boy who liked to catch bugs and chase me around the yard. But you two always did everything together and he's always liked you a lot. Why do you think it's so ridiculous to consider him for your secret admirer?"

Emma knew by the sound of her voice that Malia really wanted to know.

"Because . . ." she began, then hesitated. "Because he's Matt, that's all. He's my friend, has been my friend forever. But not that kind of friend. You know that, Malia. Mom knows that. I can't believe that even *she* suggested he might be the one."

She thought she heard Malia say "see," but she couldn't be sure as there was a lot of noise on her end. The twins must be demanding her attention, something Malia had told her happened with annoying frequency whenever she picked up the phone.

Emma continued, sure Malia was listening. "I just can't see Matt doing it, Malia. It would be like having my brother send me a dozen roses. And Matt is nothing if not practical. You should hear what he has to say about the romance novels I read. You'd think I was reading pure garbage. But they aren't that at all, of course, and I keep telling him that. Romance novels are great books—well written with wonderful characters."

"You don't have to convince me." Malia laughed. "I like a nice romance myself, but I don't get much chance to read with the twins around."

Malia's voice grew dim as she apparently moved the telephone away from her mouth to speak to the twins. She was back within a minute, returning to their conversation as though she'd never left it.

"But I don't see why you should hold it against Matt that he doesn't like romance novels. Most men don't."

"Oh, it's not just that. I mean that he's more the practical sort of guy, that's all. Computers and science and all that. He might send a plant, but not cut flowers. He thinks they're a waste of money," she explained. "It wouldn't occur to him to have dinner by candlelight, or to send special little romantic gifts."

She could hear Malia's voice speaking to the children, could hear their voices too. She waited for Malia to return to their conversation.

"Sorry, the girls were fighting over some doll clothes. I think I have the situation in hand though.

"But as to Matt, I don't know why you think he's not romantic. Isn't he the same guy who took you to the prom at the last minute because your date punked out on you? And didn't he arrive at the door with an absolutely gorgeous ginger lei because he remembered that you'd once said ginger leis were your favorite?"

"Well, yeah." Malia's words made Emma stop and think. "I guess that was romantic. Kind of."

"You just have a mental block about Matt because you've been friends for so long."

"Do you think so?"

"Yes, I do. You just stop and think about it sometime."

Emma could hear high-pitched voices in the background, growing louder. And then an ear-piercing shriek.

"Oops. Got to go. Courtney just swung her doll at Carrie's head."

Emma offered a quick goodbye and slowly replaced the receiver, considering what Malia had said. She'd have to do some serious thinking about her relationship with Matt.

The phone rang.

And she would think about it too. Just as soon as she had some time to do it.

She reached eagerly for the phone. Maybe *this* time it was the long-awaited call from her secret admirer.

It wasn't, though, as she quickly discovered. Just another friend anxious to discuss the possibilities.

The following week passed swiftly for Emma, and she never did find the time to devote to thinking about Matt.

At work, every male customer was a potential candidate for secret admirer. The thing she loved most about her job was working with the public, and now the interaction was even more exciting. Every flirtatious word, every admiring look, was cause for grave consideration.

At breaks and during their free moments, she and Kim discussed the possibilities. As the youngest member of the staff, Corinne was eager to join in their speculation. Talking about men was the thing she liked best anyway. But even Sandy, cynical about men since her divorce, was interested in Emma and her gift. And

Nishiko offered support as well, never scolding them when talk turned away from business and toward Emma's romantic Valentine's Day surprise.

In fact, it was Nishiko who suggested the mystery man might be someone from the main branch of the bank. At the surprised silence that greeted her remark, Nishiko reminded Emma and the others about the visitor they'd had early in February.

"Remember? The human resources person—he went over the new benefit plan with us? His name was Gilbert Lucas and he stayed a whole week. When he arrived, we thought he would only be here for a day or two. I really think he showed a special interest in you, Emma," Nishiko told her with a discerning smile.

Everyone quickly took to recounting memories of Gil's visit. It gave Emma something new to mull over, and she could hardly wait to talk it over with Matt.

On Saturday morning, Emma met Matt for their usual weekend tennis game. Her spirits high, she ran indefatigably over the court, returning whatever he sent her way.

Afterward, they sat together on the courtside bench, sipping from water bottles, toweling dampness from their tired bodies.

Matt wiped his forehead with a long white towel, then draped it around his neck. Emma looked at the damp-darkened hair drifting over his forehead, tickling the tops of his ears. He had beautiful ears, smooth and well-shaped, held close to his head. He hadn't gone in for the earring craze, though he would look pretty sexy with a gold stud in his ear . . .

Emma blinked. Good grief. She was starting to think like her paperback novels. Maybe Matt was right about their effect on her. She might enjoy the fantasy heroes in her books, but Matt was very real. She could feel the heat of his body radiating toward her as they sat together on the bench, could smell the masculine aroma of sweat mixed with the spicy scent of his cologne—a very appealing combination.

Her breath caught in her chest, and her mouth turned dry. Oh, yes, he was real all right. She grabbed at her water bottle and tipped it up to her mouth. The water relieved the dryness in her throat, but not the tightness in her chest. And she could still smell the titillating scent of that cologne.

Emma suddenly realized that Matt was talking to her and she had absolutely no idea what he'd said.

"What was that?"

Matt smiled at her. A speculative smile.

Speculative? *Oh, Emma, get a grip!*

"You looked a million miles away," Matt said. "What were you thinking about?"

Oh, *auwe*, as her grandmother used to say. If he heard what she'd been thinking, he'd be on her again about her reading. She forced a smile. And lied. Sort of.

"Just thinking how I could have beaten you that last set if you hadn't cheated on the line calls."

Matt stopped his water bottle halfway to his lips. "What?! I don't cheat!"

"I guess I could give you the benefit of the doubt." Emma threw him a pert smile that she knew would soothe any offense she may have caused by her teasing. It worked. Matt offered a wry smile in return.

Emma threw her racket and balls into her bag, tossed her towel on top, and zipped it closed. Better to get off the bench right away and put a little distance between the two of them. Already a light breeze was cooling her overheated body and displacing that tantalizing spicy scent with the perfume of tropical blooms from the nearby plumeria trees.

"Want to go over to the Dairy Queen and get a drink?" Matt asked. "You were going to tell me about Nishiko's idea of who your secret admirer is."

"Yeah, great." Emma almost heaved a sigh of relief. The Dairy Queen had small picnic-type tables; they could sit opposite one another and have their drinks and talk. It wouldn't be considered unusual on her part to sit across from him instead of beside him, because that's the way everyone sat there. It was the way *they* always sat there.

Relaxing at the thought that she would no longer have to sit so close to him, she started off without even waiting for Matt to finish packing up his gear.

"Race you there!"

* * *

It didn't take them long to settle down with their drinks at a small table at the Dairy Queen. They did have to spend a few minutes making a round of the tables and visiting with those who were already there. A small town didn't have too many gathering places, and in theirs the DQ was the prime spot. The picnic tables lined both sides of the building and the teens generally grouped on one side and the adults and younger children on the other.

Emma had to answer numerous inquiries about her secret admirer and whether she'd learned his identity. She answered with a simple no, not wanting to get into lengthy explanations about possibilities with everyone in town. She'd save her speculations for her conversations with Matt.

To her surprise, more than one person accused Matt of being the secret admirer. She noticed that he looked embarrassed, and his cheeks turned red under his heavy tan. It made her wonder. Why would it disconcert him to have people ask if he was the one? Did he think it so unlikely that he would send flowers that it ruined his image of himself?

Yet why else would it embarrass him to have someone think he'd sent her flowers?

Emma couldn't come to a solution to her questions. Men were just too confusing for a simple country girl like herself to understand.

Finally, they were seated together and in a position to have a private conversation.

"So," Matt began. "Tell me about Nishiko's candidate for your secret admirer." He whipped the paper cover off his plastic straw and stuck the straw into his milkshake.

Emma spoke eagerly, ignoring her soda. "Well, back at the beginning of the month, the main office in Hilo sent a human resources person out to tell us about some new benefits." She finally tore the paper covering around her straw, pushing the plastic straw into her drink, and taking a long sip of the cold soda. As she drank, she tucked in a curl that had fallen out of the elastic holding her hair back. "A few weeks ago this guy, Gilbert Lucas, drove in every day for a week."

"All the way from Hilo?"

"Yes. He was a nice person. We all liked him. He explained all the changes in the benefits plan. He asked about our jobs, observed what we did on a typical day."

"So what makes Nishiko think he's the one?"

Emma shrugged, but her eyes were bright with excitement. "I think it's intuition, actually, because she can't seem to explain it very well; though she seems to think he extended his visit from a few days to a week because he liked being around me. And there was something about the way he looked at me . . ."

Matt was unsuccessful at hiding his smile.

"And once she mentioned it, everyone else started to remember him, and finding little things to support her idea." She twirled the straw around in her cup and looked deep into Matt's eyes. "So, what do you think?"

"Sounds as good as any other theory to me. But why hasn't he called?"

"Well, Nishiko thinks he's waiting until he comes back again. He's scheduled to return sometime next month. Something about a class we can take to help us do our jobs better." She sighed at the thought of an evening of class on dull financial issues. "Anyway, he's coming back, just for a day this time."

"Sounds like a possibility," he admitted.

Matt looked into her lovely face. Her cheeks were still flushed from their recent exercise, giving her a healthy glow. Her eyes sparkled with excitement. He smiled.

"I guess you'll find out sometime next month."

Emma's eyes widened as she stared across the table at him. "Well, don't you have any opinions as to whether or not it might be him? Warnings about men with evil intentions? Requests to meet him and give your okay?"

By the time she finished her list they were both laughing.

"Hey, I don't know the guy. And you warned me off last time when I wanted to vette Lance, remember?"

She sighed. "Well, gee, thanks a lot."

"Hey, I'm trying to be supportive here," he protested.

"Sometimes you are supportive," she corrected him. "You haven't been any help at all about this secret admirer business. And I thought you'd have some good ideas, being a guy and all."

"But I'm such an unromantic guy."

Emma's eyes narrowed as she looked across the table at him. His eyes were innocence itself, but his tone indicated he didn't mean his statement literally. But was he being sarcastic, or what? He'd never claimed to be the romantic type. At least not that she recalled. Was he getting touchy about her calling him on it?

Emma returned to her drink, her eyes thoughtful as they tipped up to watch Matt.

Could Malia and the others be right? Could Matt be a candidate for secret admirer?

Chapter Five

For the next week, Emma bided time waiting for the return visit of Gilbert Lucas, wondering if he would truly turn out to be her secret admirer. Her birthday approached, but the excitement she usually felt was tempered by her continuing preoccupation with the gift of Valentine roses and her search for the identity of the sender. She spent her evenings in her room, lounging on her bed, listening to romantic music, reading her romance novels, and playing with the dried remains of her once beautiful roses. She had pressed some of them in her heaviest college textbooks, and was trying to decide on a pleasing arrangement for the dried flowers. Once that was achieved, she planned to put them in a frame to hang on the wall opposite her bed. There she would continue to enjoy them for a long time.

Her birthday dawned clear and dry, with every promise of beautiful weather for the entire day. Emma donned her prettiest dress, a deep blue rayon sprinkled with flowers in a light shade of lavender pink. She was having her breakfast of toast and coffee when the back door opened and Matt appeared.

"Happy Birthday!"

A wide smile on her face, Emma stood to greet him and was soon engulfed in a bear hug. He was big and warm and solid, and Emma wished he would never let her go. Why did they call this a "bear" hug anyway? Wouldn't a bear be big and soft and furry, not hard and muscular and smelling like sunshine and the outdoors?

Matt released her and Emma reluctantly removed her arms from around his back and stepped away.

"I have a little something for you," he informed her.

It was the first time she noticed that he had embraced her with only one arm. The other was hidden behind his back. He grinned at her, turning slightly as she leaned to the side, trying to peek.

Sonia arrived at that moment, wrapped in a faded cotton robe, and greeted them both. Before they could return her good mornings, though, she had enclosed

Emma in her arms, hugging her daughter and wishing her a happy birthday.

When she stepped back, her hands still on her daughter's upper arms, there were tears in her eyes.

"Oh, it seems like just yesterday I brought you home from the hospital. Your Daddy was so proud—two beautiful little girls." Her eyes turned toward Matt. "Bernie was so jealous. She wanted another baby too, you know. And she would have loved a little girl."

Matt nodded. "I know Mom always said she wanted more kids. I never knew why she didn't have any more after me, though."

"They thought there was some scarring caused by the C-section she had for you," Sonia told him as she moved toward the pot to pour her coffee. "They took you out in a hurry because the cord was wrapped around your neck, and she and her doctor later suspected something happened then. But she and Will didn't have the money to try any of the procedures the obstetrician recommended that may have helped her conceive again."

Emma noticed that Matt looked as surprised as she did at the news her mother had so casually dropped.

Sonia, a mug of coffee in her hand, returned to the table, not seeming to notice the reactions her tale had produced. She sat down and blew lightly at the steam rising from the mug.

"So, did you come over to wish Emma a happy birthday?" she asked Matt.

"Yes."

Matt shook his head slightly, clearing it of these new revelations. His mother had always told him she regretted his lack of siblings, but he'd never heard this story before. And since Sonia Lindsey was his mother's best friend, he believed everything she'd just said was the truth. He felt almost guilty—his birth had been the reason she couldn't have more children. Perhaps that was why she had never told him.

With Sonia's distracting disclosure, Matt almost forgot the spray of orchids hidden behind his back. Now he brought them forward and handed them to Emma with a little bow.

"An early gift," he told her. "I thought you could wear them in your hair." He glanced over her figure, taking in the deep blue of her dress with its pinkish flowers. "I had a feeling you'd be wearing that today."

Emma's cheeks turned a becoming pink, and she reached for the stem of orchids. The dendrobiums were the exact shade of the flowers on her dress, though the latter were some type of idealistic flower, unidentifiable as a real species. Still, the lavender pink of the dendrobium petals were a perfect match.

Emma leaned forward and bestowed a kiss on Matt's cheek.

"Thank you, Matt," she murmured. His intriguing scent, fresh and outdoorsy but all man, washed over her as she felt the rough texture of his unshaven cheek through the sensitive skin of her lips.

She felt a bit shaky when she moved back, and rested her free hand on the back of the chair for support.

"That was real special of you, Matt," Sonia observed. "Real special," she repeated, watching her daughter with interest.

Matt cast a worrisome glance at Sonia. Did she know that his plant of this particular type was still budding? There wasn't any way for her to know that he'd called three friends before he'd found someone who had a spray ready to cut. Or that he'd gotten up at five that morning to drive over to Keauhou to get it. Was there?

Emma caught a strange look pass from Sonia to Matt and wondered if he'd taken the blossoms from one of her plants. But that was silly. Matt had dozens of orchid plants of his own.

Emma dismissed thoughts of where he'd gotten the flowers and tried to find a logical explanation for her strange reaction to Matt's closeness. And her recent sensitivity to his cologne. Maybe she was coming down with something. Sandy had complained of a stomach ailment last week. How long did it take to come down with the flu after you'd been exposed? Would that make someone more sensitive to odors?

Deciding that she needed some distance from Matt's newly compelling presence, she started to flee the room. She paused in the doorway long enough to explain her action to the others.

"I'll go pin these in my hair." She waved the stem of blossoms she held. "Thanks again, Matt."

"Wait!"

Matt's voice stopped her before she could escape down the hall. With a deep swallow, she turned to face him once more.

"I have to go. I'm driving into Kona today and I have to leave soon. I'll see you tonight, but I wanted to give you those this morning and wish you a great day."

Emma flew back across the room, surprising herself and Matt as she threw her arms around him and gave him a quick hug and another kiss. Sonia just smiled.

"Thank you so much, Matt."

Emma stepped back, far enough away from him so that she could no longer feel the heat that always seemed to radiate from his body. If only she could distance herself from the fresh spicy scent of him as easily.

"Drive carefully."

He raised an eyebrow at this last advice, but assured her he would and left the house.

Emma could see that her mother was ready to say something, but she really didn't want to hear it. Sonia was convinced Matt had sent the original bouquet, and Emma felt certain her mother would use this latest gift to bolster her theory. Sonia wouldn't understand the difference between an expensive bouquet ordered from a florist and a spray of orchids picked from a backyard. Emma rushed from the room to pin the flowers in her hair before her mother had a chance to make a comment.

"Don't want to be late for work," she called over her shoulder.

She missed the smile of contentment that graced Sonia's face as she brought the mug to her lips.

Emma had a lot of time to reflect on Matt's sweetness and generosity that day. She'd pulled her hair on top of her head and pinned the orchids along the right side of her face, down to the piled-up hair at the back of her head. Curly tendrils fell from the clip that secured most of the hair, twisting in long ringlets along the column of her neck. Even she had admitted that it was an attractive arrangement. It seemed that everyone who saw her commented on her hair and the lovely flowers and how well they matched her dress.

Kim brought in a cake and set it in the break room, and they all helped themselves to it during their various breaks and lunch periods. Emma wondered if she was experiencing a sugar high, as she was so upbeat. She didn't think she'd been so happy since Valentine's Day, when the roses had been presented to her.

The tellers were all busy with customers when Luana entered the bank. Just as before, she bore her clipboard and a beautiful floral arrangement. But this time, everyone looked immediately toward Emma, anxious to see her reaction.

Emma, like the others, had her gaze fixed on the still-open doorway. The smile she'd been offering her customer disappeared as she stared in awe at the beauty of the bouquet Luana carried. As Luana handed it over the counter, Emma buried her nose in the blossoms—a headily fragrant mixed bouquet of pink blooms, all of which complemented her dress and the orchids in her hair. She could hardly bear to take her eyes off the beautiful bouquet long enough to sign Luana's receipt.

Her fingers trembled as she opened the small envelope. All eyes in the bank were trained on Emma's window as she removed the little card and read what was written there.

"Happy Birthday from a secret admirer."

Her voice was soft, disappointment evident in it, but everyone present heard what she said.

Standing at Emma's window, Mr. Jardine beamed at her. He was one of her favorite customers, an elderly man who came into the bank at least twice a week. Some of his transactions could easily have been handled on the telephone, but she knew he liked to get out and see people. As she apologized for the delay and counted out his money, he winked at her.

"Better treat me nice, sweetie. I may be the one sending those posies."

Emma was sure her mouth dropped open. She definitely fumbled the bills in her hand and had to restack and recount them. Mr. Jardine was an absolutely lovable old man. But the key word there was old. He was seventy if he was a day.

Later that afternoon, as she drank some tea on her break, she pondered the possibility that Mr. Jardine was indeed her secret admirer. She knew he was a widower. And if celebrities were any indication, older men often went after much younger women. Oh, dear. It almost took the joy out of the beautiful bouquet. But not quite. After all, this was Malino, not Hollywood.

Emma bit into one of the homemade coconut candies her Aunty Joy had dropped off for her birthday, scolding herself all the while. If she ate all the goodies that had been delivered to the bank today, she'd be so fat she wouldn't have to worry about a secret admirer! Still, Aunty Joy would expect a report on the quality of her candy.

As she savored the rich flavor, Emma turned her thoughts back to Gil. She hoped he returned soon, and that he did turn out to be the one sending the flowers. She didn't think she could handle this wondering for much longer.

Then a thought hit her with such force the tea in her mug sloshed up almost to the rim. If there had been a half-inch more liquid in the cup, she would have had tea all over her favorite dress. But this could be the clue that solved the mystery!

She quickly cleaned up her mug, disposed of the paper plate from the piece of cake she'd been unable to resist, and, with apologies to Aunty Joy, tossed out the last bite of candy. Then she rushed back to her spot at the counter.

At the window beside her, Kim was just finishing up with Jenny Tran. A maid at one of the hotels on the Kohala coast, Jenny came in every week to cash her paycheck. She smiled over at Emma, offering her sympathy over the continued mystery of the secret admirer. Then she wished her a happy birthday and told her how lovely her new bouquet was.

Emma smiled, thanked Jenny, and watched her exit the bank. Then she turned to Kim, anxious to bring up her new idea. The bank was temporarily empty of customers.

"How does everyone know it's my birthday?" she asked. "How did my secret admirer know?"

Kim gave her a wry smile and gestured toward the "Happy Birthday" banner she had hung that morning before Emma's arrival. "Everyone knows because of that," she said. "And since we don't know who your secret admirer is, how can we know how he found out?"

Emma stared at the large banner. It was a reflection of her state of mind that she had forgotten it was there.

"What if it's Gil? How could he have known?"

"Oh, that's easy." Nishiko was behind the counter

with them looking for some forms she needed. "Gil could get it from your personnel file. He's in human resources, remember, and they have your file at the main branch."

"Oh." Emma's shoulders slumped as she realized that knowledge of her birth date would not eliminate anyone after all. She sniffed at the flowers again, something she'd been doing since they had arrived. The bouquet included carnations and lilies and the scent was wonderful. Not as sensually enticing as roses perhaps, but rather exotic and interesting all the same. And the spicy scent lent by the carnations recalled the spiciness of a man's cologne . . .

She straightened the T-leaf lei Kim had given her that morning and sat up tall on her stool. "Mr. Jardine actually suggested it might be him," she told the others.

Kim laughed, quickly joined by Nishiko. Corinne, on the other side of Kim, giggled.

"Mr. Jardine?" Corinne said. "That short, thin little old man?" She giggled again. "Oh, Emma, what if it is him?"

They all laughed, even Emma, though she wasn't sure it was really funny. If poor Mr. Jardine really did have a crush on her, how on earth could she let him down without hurting his feelings? He really was a sweet old dear.

"Say, maybe he's rich? Have you ever noticed what his account balances are like?"

Nishiko cast a stern look toward Corinne, who quickly found a task that needed her immediate attention.

Emma, who had known Mr. Jardine for a long time, knew that he was comfortable in his retirement, but not rich. In fact, she didn't think she knew of anyone in Malino who could be called "rich" as she thought of that term. "Rich" was someone who had enough money to never worry about bills, someone who could purchase clothes on a whim without thought to the cost. "Rich" was movie stars, and celebrities, and tourists from the mainland who stayed at the Four Seasons Hualalai or the Mauna Kea Beach Hotel for a month at a time.

Emma contemplated her beautiful flowers one more time. Would her admirer have to be rich to afford these gifts?

She just didn't know.

Emma's mother had arranged a potluck dinner party for Emma's birthday, so it was late that evening before Emma and Matt were able to find time to be alone together. Throughout the evening, speculation on the identity of the secret admirer was the prime topic of conversation. All the single men were accused of being such, and even a few married ones after the accusers had had a beer—or two or three.

So Matt had already heard all about the new gift long before Emma had a chance to tell him about it herself. She sat with his gift in her hand, a grouping of lifelike yellow porcelain roses gathered on top of a little trinket bowl. When she raised the lid, "Memories" began to play. She was so thrilled with the gift, she'd carried it over to Matt's house with her.

"The flowers are absolutely the most beautiful thing, Matt," she finished. Her fingertips traced over the porcelain roses of her new gift, giving the sentence a double entendre. "I decided to leave them at work so that I can enjoy them for the rest of the week."

Matt smiled quietly, enjoying her recitation of earlier events. After all the food and drinks at the party, they were sitting together on his lanai, bundled into sweaters with warm mugs of chocolate nearby. Poki lay contented at their feet. They had wanted to help clean up the mess at Emma's, but Sonia and Kim had sent them firmly on their way, saying that the birthday girl should *not* have to handle any of the clean-up. Matt got off by dint of his association with her.

Matt shifted a little in his chair so that he could see Emma's face. There was just enough light from the kitchen window to highlight her features.

"Are you any closer to identifying the mystery man? You have two clues now."

"I know, and it's driving me batty. Mr. Jardine actually suggested he might be the one. You know Mr. Jardine." Emma realized that was one of the nice things about living in a small town. Everyone knew everyone else. Even if you'd been away for several years, the way both Emma and Matt had been, you still knew everyone. So when speaking about the townspeople, you didn't have to take the time to explain who they were. "He's a wonderful old dear and I love him. But he must be seventy years old!"

Her voice rose on the final words and she snapped the lid of her music box closed, cutting off the tinkle of the song. And Matt laughed. Emma looked indignant.

"Well, I'm glad you find my life so funny."

"I'm not laughing at you, Emma. It's the picture of you and Mr. Jardine, out on a date . . ." He laughed again. "Now this *is* funny."

Emma couldn't help herself. She had to join in. It was a ridiculous picture. Poki, hearing their laughter, jumped up, ready to play, and they had to take a few minutes to settle him back down.

"Don't those books you like so much ever have a big age difference between the man and the woman?"

Emma fidgeted in her chair. Matt was always criticizing her reading choice. But he had an uncanny way of knowing precisely what type of material was in them.

"The age differences aren't *that* large. Except in the historicals. And even then the heroine might be twenty and the hero thirty or thirty-five. Not twenty-three and seventy for goodness sake."

"So who knows that today is your birthday?"

She sighed. "I thought that would be the key too. It seemed like such a brilliant notion. But Kim put up this big banner at the bank. And Nishiko said that Gil could have found out easily through the personnel records in his office. So knowing my birthday doesn't eliminate anyone at all."

Too restless to sit still a moment longer, Emma rose and began to pace. She still held the little music box in her hands. Poki quickly fell into step behind her, watching her hands anxiously in the hope that they held a toy for him.

But Emma's mind was far from doggy games.

"How could he know it's my birthday and not bother to call?! I'm beginning to think it's hopeless. If this guy doesn't call me and reveal himself tonight, I may *never* know who it is." Her voice rose to a high pitch, and she swung her arms out in frustration. "And it's getting pretty late for a phone call," she added with a quick glance at her watch.

Matt watched her, ready to catch his fragile gift if it left the safety of her grasp. Her pacing was full of repressed energy that seemed to radiate outward from her slim body. Her hands waved gracefully around her as she spoke, gesturing to emphasize her words. He never understood why she didn't knock over lamps and small tables when she prowled through a room. But she sailed past furniture without touching any of it, and never tripped over anything either.

Out here on the lanai she managed to avoid both the orchids hanging from the edge of the roof, and the potted crotons that lined the edge of the concrete slab. And she never collided with Poki, who stayed at her heels.

Matt especially enjoyed the way she continued to cradle the little music box; his gift had been the obvious favorite among all the various things she'd received that night.

"Maybe I sent them."

Because of the darkness and her preoccupied thoughts, Emma didn't even look his way. She didn't note the speculative tone. She never missed a step.

"Don't be silly. It's just not your style."

She stopped pacing and stood in front of him. Poki stopped too, looking up at her to see what she would do next. Absently, she opened the box, releasing a few lines of "Memories."

"Besides, we've been talking about this since Valentine's Day. I'd know by now if it was you."

Matt had to grin. "So, you can read my mind, can you?"

"More or less. And you read mine. You know we do. We always have. That's what other people don't understand, and why it would never work between us. How can there be any magic between two people who know each other so well?"

Emma had used up most of her energy and plopped back down in her chair. The tinkling of the music box continued, but the wooden slats of the chair groaned. Poki whined and Matt winced, but apparently Emma wasn't affected. She closed the music box and set it carefully on the table, then reached for her chocolate, sipping it tentatively to see if it was still warm. She wrinkled her nose and set it aside, turning to face Matt.

Poki gave up on Emma playing with him and decided to join Matt, pushing his golden head beneath his master's hand.

"We always have been in sync, haven't we, Emma?" His voice was soft. "In fact, we're perfect together."

Emma looked startled. Then she seemed to relax and smiled. "Of course. We have a perfect friendship." She reached across and laid her hand on top of his, resting on the arm of his chair. "I don't know what I'd do without you, Matt."

Despite the coolness of the night, Matt's hand exuded warmth. Heat quickly engulfed Emma's hand, and began to creep up her arm. Her fingers tingled with it, and she had the oddest craving to run them lightly up his arm, across the back of his neck, through the short hairs there, and up into his thick curls. He did have the nicest head of hair!

Startled at her strange thoughts, Emma pulled her hand back to her own chair. She fumbled with the fabric of her skirt, smoothing it over her lap, then pulling it over her knees. Finally she reached for the trinket box again, and opened the cover. The sweet melody filled the sudden and unusual silence between them.

Matt watched Emma play with her skirt, then busy her hands with the music box once again. She was disconcerted about something, but darned if he knew what. Could it be that her touch on his hand had affected her as much as it had him? He'd felt the soft touch of her smooth fingers all the way to his toes. Her nearness affected him, too. And her scent.

Her scent. Just thinking about it made him hot. It didn't even have to be that perfume she wore, the one that smelled like gardenias. He liked the way she smelled of soap and shampoo when she rushed over after her bath to tell him something. He liked the musky scent that surrounded her after their tennis matches on hot tropical mornings. He liked the way she smelled of salt and sun after swimming in the sea.

Matt's hand closed into a fist, and he moved his arm into his lap. He took his other hand from Poki's head and covered the spot where Emma's touch had burned into his flesh. He could still feel her fingers, butterfly soft as they rested on his. His heart still beat a rapid thump-thump, the after-effect of the brief touch of his unlikely butterfly.

He stifled an overwhelming urge to sigh. Emma might not know what she would do without him. But she didn't seem to know what she ought to do *with* him either.

Matt was brought back into the present when Emma closed the trinket box with a snap, cutting off the melody in the midst of a held note. Her pretty mouth was turned down at the corners.

"Here it is March fifth already," she moaned. "And I still don't know who sent the Valentine's Day roses!"

"Yeah," Matt agreed. "I can't believe it either."

Chapter Six

"Matt. Matt. How do I look?"

Matt heard Emma's voice long before he saw her. Since her birthday, Emma had talked of nothing but the visit of the elusive Gil Lucas. For most of the hour they'd spent at the Dairy Queen after their tennis match on Saturday morning, she'd done little but worry over what she would say to him and how she should act. She'd spent the rest of the time wondering what he might say to her when they finally met again.

So now, on the day of his fateful return visit, Emma had come over to see Matt. He savored the thought that she needed his support before embarking on this important day. Even though she was actually using him to try to attract another man.

"There you are!"

Emma stood in the doorway of his bedroom, sounding exasperated. But really, where did she expect him to be at six o'clock in the morning? He'd just gotten up, and was barely dressed when he first heard her calling his name.

"I let Poki out," she added.

Matt hurriedly pulled his T-shirt over his head, then ran his fingers through his hair rather than go back into the bathroom for his comb. Just in case she followed him in there too. The bathroom was too small to share with Emma.

"Emma." He could be exasperated too. "You shouldn't be walking into a man's bedroom like that. I might have been changing."

Emma, her mouth half open, ready to speak again, closed it abruptly and stood very still. Her heart pounded, blood rushed to her head, and her breath caught in her throat.

"Emma. Are you all right?"

Matt reached her in two long steps, putting his hands on her upper arms. He peered into her glassy eyes.

"Good grief, Emma. What's the matter?"

Emma blinked, but she still couldn't breathe. She could feel the heat that always seemed to be stored in his body—it was flowing through his hands into her arms, traveling quickly through her body via the blood rushing double time through her veins. She could hear a roaring in her ears that she knew was the sound of her own blood.

She was so hot!

Matt was still holding her, steering her toward the bed. Good grief, not the bed! It didn't take much to visualize him reclining on the bed.

Emma finally managed an adequate breath, could actually feel the oxygen entering her system and pumping through her. If only she could keep breathing calmly, she thought, the cool oxygen would dissipate some of the heat.

They had reached the bed, and Matt pushed her down until she sat on the edge of the mattress. Then he removed his hands from her arms. But before she could breathe a sigh of relief, he put one hand on the back of her neck and pressed her head down toward her ankles. Emma's hands shot out as she struggled to keep her seat.

"Matt, stop! What are you doing?"

"Are you okay?" He leaned down until his eyes were level with her own and examined her face carefully. "You looked like you were going to faint or something."

"Of course I'm okay." She took a few careful breaths to be certain it was the truth. The thunder in her ears had ceased, her heart was returning to its normal steady rate. Now that he was no longer touching her. "I've never fainted in my life and I'm not going to start now. What's gotten into you?"

He reached for her again, and she pushed his hands away, slapping at him playfully. She couldn't let that happen again, but how on earth could she explain it to him? Instead she stood, glared at him, and headed for the door.

"I'm not supposed to be in your bedroom, remember?" She adopted as icy a tone as possible, and flounced from the room.

Matt followed. But he didn't smile. Something was seriously wrong.

When they arrived in the kitchen, Matt was relieved to see that the coffeemaker, set on a timer, was just completing its cycle. He needed that shot of caffeine this morning.

Emma, restless as always, pulled the mugs from the cupboard and poured out two cupfuls. Matt sat down, accepted the mug from her, took a long sip even though it scalded the roof of his mouth, then looked into her eyes. His scowl was a combined reaction to the burn and Emma's strange behavior.

"Tell me what the heck happened in there."

Emma, too anxious to sit, put down her mug and walked toward the windows and back again. Poki barked and she opened the door to let him back in before retracing her steps.

"I don't know. I'm so excited about Gil coming in today. I guess it's just nerves. I couldn't eat breakfast," she added.

And please, God, she prayed, let him believe that. Because I don't know what's going on here, but I don't think I'm ready to try and figure it out this morning.

Matt muttered something she couldn't quite make out, and she stopped in front of the table, reaching for her mug and taking a delicate sip.

"Hmm, you always have the best coffee." She took another sip before setting the mug back on the table.

"But, Matt, the reason I came over here was to see how you liked this dress."

She stepped back, away from the table so that he could see all of her outfit. Putting one foot in front of the other in the classic model's pose, she took a small step forward, twirled, then twirled again. She put her hands on her hips and looked at him, raising her brows in inquiry.

"So, what do you think?"

Matt never took his eyes off her. She wore a dress the color of red wine, with narrow black lines running through it. The fabric skimmed over her body's curves stopping short of her knees, showing off those cute calves and shapely ankles. The style was deceptively simple and deeply flattering. She was exquisite, is what he thought. What would she say if he told her that? Would she laugh, then say, "no seriously"? Probably.

"You look terrific, as always, Emma. I've always liked that dress. The red makes your cheeks glow."

Emma's eyes lost some of their sparkle, edged out by panic as she rushed for the bathroom and its mirror. "My cheeks are too red?" she cried.

Matt sighed. No matter what he said, she was going to take it the wrong way. He rose from the table and trailed after her.

"Emma, your cheeks are not too red. You look wonderful. Your cheeks are pink, a nice healthy pink. Lots of women use rouge to get that same pretty pink glow."

"You think?" Her head came around the doorway, then disappeared inside once more.

"Come on out of there. I'll make some scrambled eggs."

He started back toward the kitchen.

"Oh, I can't eat." Emma's laugh was nervous, self-deprecating. "I'm so nervous, I feel like I might throw up."

He was already reaching under the cupboard for a pan when she admitted that. He straightened, looked her over, then closed the cupboard door. Despite her rosy cheeks, she did look a little ill. Instead, he went to the pantry and pulled out a box.

"I've got just the thing. Instant oatmeal." He waved the box in her direction as he reached for a bowl. "Makes up in no time in the microwave."

Emma approached him and took the box out of his hands.

"Thanks, Matt. I really appreciate it. But I couldn't possibly eat this morning."

She ran her hands down her body, straightening the drape of her dress. Matt thought he would die watching those hands. How he wished they were *his* hands touching her in that intimate fashion. His touch would be so light, so gentle. Her skin would tingle until her whole body was as rosy as her cheeks.

Matt felt his own cheeks flushing and forced his mind back to the kitchen. He realized he'd missed something Emma had just said.

"What was that?"

Emma frowned at him. "Honestly, Matt. I said, you're sure I look all right?"

"You look beautiful."

It was such a simple, heartfelt comment she couldn't possibly disbelieve him. A bright smile eased the worry from her face.

"Will you be here tonight when I get home from work? I'll come right over to tell you how it went."

Matt nodded. His face was solemn, but he didn't think Emma noticed. She raced out the door, ready for work a whole hour early. She'd go home now and fidget for a while, bother Sonia for opinions she'd disregard, then she'd leave for the bank and arrive there much too early.

Matt returned to the table, sat down heavily, and gulped the rest of his coffee in one long swallow. How had such a simple plan to win her love gone so terribly wrong? He looked at Poki sitting patiently beside him.

"I wish you could talk, Poki. We could have a serious man-to-man about Emma and women in general."

Poki seemed to nod in agreement.

"Aw, heck, what would you know about that stuff anyway," he mumbled, remembering that poor Poki had been neutered. "Though I think Emma might like you better than she likes me."

With a deep sigh he got up to get Poki his breakfast.

The Emma that entered his kitchen that evening was as far from the woman of the morning as the ocean was from the mountain. The morning Emma had been bubbling with excitement, her dress fresh and crisp, her eyes sparkling. This evening, she was downcast, her dress limp and wrinkled, her eyes clouded. If she were the crying type, Matt knew she would be sobbing already.

"So it wasn't him, huh?"

Emma pulled out a chair and dropped gracelessly into it. Poki quickly put his head into her lap in his own unique way of offering comfort.

"How'd you know?"

Matt couldn't help it. He had to laugh. The deep rumble echoed around the buttercup yellow walls, momentarily drowning out the rich tones of Sonny Chillingworth's guitar playing on the radio.

Emma stared up at him, her listlessness turning to anger.

"Well, I'm glad you find it so funny."

She stared at him a moment, trying to pout the way the actresses did in the movies. But instead of turning down, her lips insisted on tipping upward. And she was soon laughing with him. Poki lifted his head, and Emma swore he was smiling too.

"I guess it was pretty funny. We were all watching him so carefully, the poor man thought there was something wrong with him. He actually asked Nishiko if he'd spilled something on his clothes that he wasn't aware of." Her laughter threatened to stop her speech. She put her hands over her mouth, took a couple of shaky breaths, and continued.

"Finally, just before lunch time, Mr. Jardine came in. I was helping him with a problem he had balancing his checkbook when he saw Gil come out of the back room with Sandy. And he looked over at him and said, in this really loud voice, 'So young man, are you Emma's secret admirer?' "

Emma's *joie de vivre* had returned. Although her cheeks were pink with embarrassment, her eyes sparkled once more and her smile was genuine.

"I thought I'd *die*. Just lie down right there on the floor behind my window and *die*. I'm sure my face was as red as my dress." Her hand fluttered over her skirt as she attempted to straighten a crease. And avoid looking into Matt's face.

"Then I looked over at Gil, trying to put an apology into my look, you know?" She abandoned her skirt and raised her eyes to meet Matt's. "And he had the strangest look on his face. Mostly surprise, I guess. And then his cheeks got all pink, these two bright round spots, like rouge on a doll's face." Her fingertips rested lightly on her own cheeks, indicating the area where Gil's had reddened. She had to laugh again.

"Oh, Matt, you should have seen his face. I thought he might be sick, right there in the lobby. Mr. Jardine took one look at him and said, 'Well guess not. Not unless you're the shyest person ever born.' And then he turned to me and said in kind of a stage whisper that could be heard all over the building, 'And then he probably wouldn't've had the gumption to send the flowers in the first place.' "

Matt was watching her, enjoying her laughter, loving the way she was caught up in the humor of the situation.

"I can't believe how funny it is now. At the time it was just embarrassing, and then all afternoon I was too humiliated to even look Gil in the eye. I even agreed to take that class because I felt so bad about the whole episode." Emma sighed. She didn't enjoy those finance classes; most of them were beyond boring.

Emma stood, pushing the chair back toward the table, and walked over to the windows. Poki trailed along behind her. Once there she started back toward Matt again.

Matt watched her, fearing that a foolish grin branded his face. But Emma was back to her old self, a tiger prowling his kitchen. If he got down on all fours and looked closely, he felt sure there would be a trail marked into the linoleum from years' worth of Emma's restless pacing. If island households followed the mainland style of wearing shoes inside the house, there would probably be a worn spot visible from across the room.

Matt felt his grin grow even wider.

"So," Emma continued, "Gil was so disconcerted about the whole thing, Nishiko had to take him aside and explain everything. About the roses on Valentine's Day and the whole secret admirer business. And she told him how the whole town has been guessing at the identity of the secret admirer."

She sat down again, slipping into the chair without even pulling it all the way out. It meant that the edge of the table squeezed against her upper body.

Matt's grin faded. He swallowed hard, his throat dry. It was a struggle to pull his gaze back upward.

Emma didn't notice. She was telling him how Gil had gotten involved, asking questions about the gifts, hearing the various theories the others had to offer.

"In the end, he thought the whole thing was pretty exciting. But I was still embarrassed. It turns out he has a girlfriend in Hilo, a teacher. They're practically engaged. That's why he was so agitated when Mr. Jardine blurted that out. It could have been the end of his job if his supervisors thought he was using his position to hit on female employees."

Emma finally seemed to notice the strange look on Matt's face.

"What's wrong with you, Matt? You look a little odd."

Matt was still wrestling to keep his straying vision away from the fabric stretched snugly across her body. He cleared his throat, but his voice remained strained.

"Ah . . . my throat's a little dry." He managed a short cough to support his statement.

"Oh." Emma bounced out of her chair. "Let me get you a drink. Water all right?"

Matt nodded, still not trusting his voice. But now that she was up again, the dress lay smoothly—and loosely—across her upper body. So he would be just fine. As soon as she stepped away from him and took her hands with her. He swallowed hard.

Emma filled a glass with ice and water, then brought it over to him. But instead of moving away again, returning to her pacing or even to her chair, she stayed beside him. And she put her hand on his forehead!

Matt gulped down the water, almost emptying the glass at one pull. The sweet scent of gardenias washed over him, further inflaming already sensitive nerve endings. Why didn't she move away from him?

"Do you feel all right otherwise, Matt?" Her fingers trailed down the side of his face to rest lightly against his throat just below his jawline. "Your glands aren't swollen. But there's some kind of flu going around, so you should take care of yourself. Maybe some vitamin C," she advised, going to the cupboard where she knew he kept his vitamins and bringing the bottle back to the table. She removed the glass from his hand and refilled it. Poki pushed his head between them, anxious to see what was happening.

Matt accepted the pills and water meekly, swallowing them quickly. When her fingers had touched his face, moving across his flesh like a hot iron, he'd almost lost control. He'd wanted to grab her, pull her down into his lap, and kiss her until she admitted that they were more than just childhood friends. She was constantly saying that she didn't know what she'd do if she didn't have him as her best friend. Why couldn't she see that she didn't have to do without him—ever?

Emma had returned to her restless roaming.

"Oh, I knew coming over here and talking to you would make me feel better. I felt just terrible before—the embarrassment over Gil finding out that way. It all came back to me in the car driving home, and I felt pretty depressed. And then I got frustrated . . . thinking I might never know who sent those roses."

She flounced over to Matt, still sitting stolidly in his chair, and gave him a quick, impetuous kiss on the cheek, squeezing his shoulders at the same time. He managed to suppress the moan that threatened—just.

"Why don't you come over and have dinner with us? Mom said to ask you. She made a pot roast, so there's plenty."

She moved toward the door, turning to see if he would follow her.

"Go on ahead," he said, his voice close to a croak. He cleared his throat, hoping to get it back to normal. "I'll just, ah . . ." He needed a few minutes to himself, but his brain just wasn't its usual keen-witted self. "I need a minute to . . ."

He couldn't think of a thing, but Emma suddenly nodded, as though she actually understood what he was stammering over.

"Oh, sure. Go ahead. I'll tell Mom you're coming."

Matt stared after her.

"What does she think I'm going to do?" he asked Poki once she'd closed the door behind her. He shrugged as if it didn't matter and downed the rest of the water in his glass. He rubbed his hand, damp from the beaded condensation on the glass, over the dog's golden head. A few deep breaths, and he felt ready to rise from the table.

"We're going to have to do something about Emma, Poki," he announced. And it would have to be soon. The woman was driving him absolutely daft.

Chapter Seven

"Malia. Is that you?"

Emma's voice rose in surprise as she cradled the phone against her ear and settled more comfortably into the pillows propped up against the headboard of her bed. The paperback book she'd been reading fell from her lap onto the bedspread. Emma didn't bother marking her place. The story was interesting but the hero paled beside her own secret admirer.

Emma glanced at the clock as she readjusted the receiver against her ear. It confirmed what she thought. It was almost nine o'clock. Not too late here in Hawaii, but *very* late in Texas. Especially for the mother of two active toddlers.

"What are you doing up at this hour?"

Malia sighed loud enough for Emma to hear. "Carrie has an ear infection and has some medicine for it. And Courtney was feeling a little jealous of the extra attention her sister was getting, so *she* started acting up. It's been a rough day."

"Oh, dear." Emma was sympathetic. "You should be in bed resting up for tomorrow."

"I'm still too tightly wound to fall asleep. And I'm curled up nicely in Ron's big ole recliner, with the afghan pulled up over me." She laughed. "I just hope I don't fall asleep while you're talking. Because I'm dying to hear the latest news about your secret admirer."

Malia's voice became soft and intimate, and Emma remembered girlish confidences in their youth. There had been too few of those times, probably because of the age difference between the girls. Emma had been more wont to confide her troubles to Matt than to her older sister, who always seemed to be busy doing important things with her own friends. But since Malia had moved to the mainland, Emma felt closer to her sister. They spent hours on the phone talking about the minutiae of their lives.

"Didn't you tell me that that man from the main branch was coming in today?" Malia asked. "I want to hear all about it."

Emma dutifully recounted the story of Gil's return to the bank, Mr. Jardine's comment, and all the rest of it. This time she could laugh from the outset, not feeling nearly so embarrassed about their red faces or

Mr. Jardine's stage whisper. Matt's reaction to the story had definitely freed her to see the absurdity of the day.

Three thousand miles away, Malia laughed too. "Oh, Emma, I'm so glad I called. It's too bad Gil wasn't the one. But I have to tell you, I feel so much better after laughing about it with you."

"You know what they say about laughter . . ."

"The best medicine," they chorused, with more laughter.

"I've got to go," Malia told her. "I'm getting so relaxed, I may not be able to get out of this chair. I'll probably fall asleep the moment I lay my head down."

"That's good. Give the girls a hug and a kiss from their Aunty Emma."

With assurances that she would, Malia hung up.

"Did she call especially to hear about Gil?"

Emma was so startled by her mother's voice, she dropped the phone on the floor and had to fumble around with her hands to find it again. When the phone was back in its proper place on her night table, Emma lounged against the headboard and looked toward the door. Sonia stood there, a cup of tea in her hands.

"That was Malia on the phone, wasn't it?" Sonia looked pointedly at the clock.

"Yes. Carrie has an ear infection and Courtney was acting up demanding equal time. So she had a rough day. She said she was too wound up to sleep once she finally got them to bed, so she called to hear an update on the secret admirer."

Sonia came into the room and sat on the end of the bed. "Maybe I should call tomorrow and talk to the girls."

She took a sip of her tea and looked closely at Emma. "Are you terribly disappointed that Gil wasn't your secret admirer?"

Emma gazed toward the far wall of the room, her staring eyes seeing only fuzzily the rows of colorful paperbacks arranged on the bookshelf there. She considered for a moment before turning back to her mother.

"I thought I was. At work, I mean, when I first realized it wasn't him. And when I was so embarrassed about Mr. Jardine blurting it out that way." She shrugged. "Gil is a nice-looking guy. Tall, lean, dark hair." She grinned at her mother. "My type."

"Hmm," was all Sonia said.

"And he has a good education and a good job."

Emma shrugged again. "But now I realize that it doesn't matter that he wasn't the one. I didn't know him before, except casually, so it's no great loss."

Sonia sipped at her tea. "Not like it would be if, say, Matt left you."

"Oh, Mom, don't even suggest such a thing!" Emma leaned forward. "You know how much our friendship means. To both of us! Matt would never leave me, as you put it. Besides, we aren't boyfriend and girlfriend. You don't *leave* a neighbor-type friend."

Sonia took another sip from her tea cup, but her eyes remained on Emma and her aspect was serious. "He's a good-looking guy, you know. Tall, lean, dark hair. Has a good education. A good job."

Emma giggled nervously. Her mother was throwing her words back at her. But to what purpose?

Sonia finished her tea and rose from the bed. She stopped in the bedroom doorway and looked back at her daughter.

"One of these days, Matt's going to get married. And his wife might not appreciate the fact that his best friend is a woman."

Emma stared after Sonia. Her lower lip trembled, but her mother was no longer there to see it.

Emma sank back into the pillows. She felt like she'd been kicked in the gut.

Matt was hunched over beneath the hedge dividing his property from the Lindsey's when he heard Sonia call out to him. He straightened, arching his back to relieve muscles achy from stooping as Poki ran over to greet their neighbor.

"I saw you working out here and thought you might like a cold drink," Sonia told him, holding up a can of his favorite soda.

"Thanks. I could use it." He popped the tab and took a long drink. "I could see some weeds from my office window, and I thought I'd take a short break and come out and pull them." He gave a wry laugh. "But there are more than I thought and it's taking *much* longer than I expected."

Sonia laughed. "That's the way it always goes. That's why I try to come out every day and do a little. I come out right after my story is done, and work for a half hour, maybe an hour."

"You still watch that soap opera, huh?" Matt grinned at her. "Is that the one Mom watched? What was it, *Fancy Life?*"

"Oh, you." Sonia waved her hand at him, dismissing what he'd said with an amused grin. "*Fancy Life*! Honestly! It's *Our Life*."

"Oh, right." Matt grinned back, unrepentant. He took another sip of soda, enjoying the quiet moment with his lifelong neighbor.

"Did you notice I'm wearing my green shirt?" Matt asked her, indicating his grass-green T-shirt decorated with an etching of Waipio Valley. "It's Saint Patrick's Day."

"Oh, I know." Sonia shook her head. "Emma ran around in a tizzy this morning because she couldn't find her green dress. And it turned out she'd washed it on Sunday so that she could wear it today, and left it hanging in the extra bathroom to dry."

"That's our Emma." Matt chuckled. "She was in such a state over Gil's visit, I'm surprised she even remembered Saint Patrick's Day was coming up."

He finished off the soda, crushed the can in his hand, and tossed it toward the trash can that sat at the corner of the lanai, Poki racing after it. It bounced off the side of the container with a loud tinny noise, then fell into it. The dog let out a bark of disappointment at being cheated out of a toy and Matt and Sonia laughed. Matt stooped to retrieve a tennis ball Poki had abandoned near him after an earlier game and tossed it across the lawn.

As Poki dashed after it, Matt turned back to Sonia and grinned. "Maybe Emma will get something green from her secret admirer today," he suggested.

Sonia looked at him long and hard. "Maybe she will."

Monday was a busy day at the bank, and when it came close to the fifteenth like St. Patrick's Day did, it was hectic. Those who got paid at mid-month were still trickling in with checks to deposit or cash, and there were the usual merchants making deposits, or getting change for the registers. So they had a very busy morning.

As Emma left—late—for her morning break, she reflected that at least everyone was in a cheerful mood. There was a lot of green around, and convivial greetings like "top o' the morning."

So she was still sitting in the break room with a cup of tea, a half-eaten shamrock cookie, and a romance novel, when Corinne barged into the little room.

"Emma, Emma. You have to come out here."

Emma, still engrossed in the lives of Baron Wolfson and Elizabeth of Woodlea, stared blankly at Corinne. Then she grinned. "Are we being robbed?"

Corinne paled. It was one of her biggest fears, that she would be at the counter when someone passed over a note saying "give me all your cash, I have a gun."

"No, of course not." Corinne's look of concern changed to a grin. "It's Luana."

Before Corinne could say more, Emma was out of her seat and pushing past her to get back into the lobby.

Luana stood at Emma's empty window, a long white lei box tied up with a green bow in her hands.

Emma released the breath she hadn't realized she'd been holding. It came out as a soft "ohhh," a sound of expectation, of awe. A sound of quiet excitement.

"Got another one for you," Luana told her with a grin. She thrust out her clipboard. "Sign here."

Emma scribbled her name, her eyes still on the box. A lei? Oh, this was too thrilling for words.

She was so excited she had trouble untying the ribbon and opening the box. As she fumbled with the tissue paper, the unique scent of *maile* floated up to her nostrils, and she knew what she would find. She parted the tissue, and stared down at the thick twisted strands of leafy vine. A string of bead-like crown flowers, white with a purplish tinge, was tucked among the vines. A small card lay snuggled into the glossy leaves. Printed across the top were the words: Happy St. Patrick's Day. Underneath it said, "A little something green for you, from your secret admirer."

"Oh."

Emma could hardly speak. It was a marvelous present. She *loved maile.* And the string of crown flowers relieved the heaviness of the green leaves and gave interest to the lei and to her green dress. She lifted the heavy strands and placed it carefully around her neck. The sweet spicy scent of the vine rose around her, and she breathed in deeply. It was heavenly.

"What's the card say?"

"Is it signed this time?"

The other workers and even the customers were crowding around her, hoping to finally learn the identity of the man. Emma shook her head.

"Still?" Kim sounded as exasperated as Emma felt.

"Boy, I wish I had an admirer like him, secret or not." Corinne's voice was so wistful the others laughed.

"It's wonderful." Emma's voice was low and heavy with emotion. "It's just wonderful."

But deep inside she was beginning to wonder. She'd about run out of possible candidates, and the excitement was turning into frustration.

Chapter Eight

Matt waited anxiously for Emma to return home from the bank. Would she have finally put together all the clues, finally figured out that her secret admirer wasn't so secret after all?

He turned off the computer and eased back in his office chair. He'd spent a lot on a good chair when he created his home office, because of the hours he spent sitting at the computer. His desk chair was almost as comfortable as his recliner.

Matt put his hand up to rub the tension from his forehead. Three years ago, who would have guessed that he'd be here, in Malino, living in the house he grew up in? Courting the girl next door in his own mysterious fashion?

Three years ago, Matt had graduated from the University of Oregon at the top of his class. He'd already made a name for himself in the electronic world by inventing the animation process that had been used to create a computer game called TygR. TygR took off like nothing seen before or since. Within weeks it was the top-selling computer game in the U.S.; within months, the world. And Matt had negotiated a percentage of the profits.

So when he graduated with honors six months after its release, Matt had offers from companies all over the world. Numerous electronic firms wanted him on board. So did game makers and animated film producers. Matt's first choice was to go into business for himself, but when one of the best firms in Silicon Valley made him an exorbitant offer, he accepted. He thought it would probably be a good idea to work for an established firm for a few years anyway. And he could invest his salary and most of the game money and be a billionaire by the time he was thirty.

It hadn't worked out quite that way. Oh, he might still be a billionaire by the time he was thirty. He tried to keep a low profile though, and no one in Malino seemed to have any idea that what he did for a living was so successful and so profitable. In the three years since his return, not one person had spoken to him about TygR.

He grinned. It was one of those win/lose situations. He was proud of his association with the game. It was successful because playing it was a good, fun experience. But the realistic animation process was the real key to its success. And he did get embarrassed when people who knew about it fawned over him. He didn't want to be known as the local celebrity; but sometimes he felt a desire to be recognized for what he'd managed to accomplish in his twenty-five years. To be more than good ole Matt from Malino.

Even Emma, dear sweet Emma, had no idea about his business success. She often asked him about his work, but he could see she didn't understand half of what he told her. He'd shown her how to play TygR, but she really wasn't interested. The game hadn't grabbed her, the way it did so many millions of others. Perhaps that was why she didn't understand how many people spent hours engrossed in TygR's intricate treasure hunts. Or realize that his small share in the game's profits amounted to hundreds of thousands of dollars a year.

Emma, bless her heart, worried about his financial future. She had suggested more than once that he do more freelance work for his old company. He'd only spent a year with them, a successful year of making contacts and learning about how the big companies operated.

And then one day his parents went out fishing, joining friends on their thirty-foot fishing boat. A sudden squall had come up, surprising even the seasoned fishermen. The boat was never seen again, lost at sea with all persons aboard.

He'd come back to Malino immediately, of course, to see what he could do. Which wasn't much. But he'd decided to give up the job and move back. There was no one else to keep up the house if they should return. In his head he knew they were gone, but in his heart he couldn't help but hope for a better ending. Perhaps he had that in common with Emma after all, she with her romance books with their universally happy endings.

So he'd moved his computers into his old home and formed his own company. He still worked on animation techniques and computer games, and he did some work for his old company. They had hated to see him go and had asked him to consider working full-time from his home. But Matt had some ideas of his own to implement, and a new game idea he wanted to develop, and he needed time to work on them.

And that was a laugh. He'd moved in here into his small home filled with memories, thinking he'd be all alone with endless time to spend at his computer. His years away at school had dulled his memory of small towns. There had been endless streams of people. First they came to welcome him home and offer sympathy on the loss of his parents. Then the mothers with single daughters began bringing him home-cooked goodies. And inviting him to share family meals or picnics. And the aunties with unwed nieces. Even one elderly woman with a granddaughter coming from Honolulu for a three-week visit.

His new game still wasn't finished, though he'd done well selling concepts for new games.

Then Emma's father had had that fatal heart attack and she had returned. They fell back into their old friendship as easily as if they had never been separated. Although they had attempted to keep in touch during their years apart, neither of them was much of a letter writer. They'd tried phone calls, but it was too difficult to coordinate their two busy schedules. Leaving short messages on answering machines wasn't satisfactory, so they'd given that up. And Emma wasn't into e-mail.

An unexpected advantage to having Emma back next door was the marked decrease in neighborly visits. Emma dashed back and forth between the houses at least once a day, just as she had when they were teens. Emma considered him her dear friend and confidante, but most of the town thought of them as a couple. So the matchmakers were staying away.

For Matt, seeing Emma again had kindled feelings far different from those he'd had in high school. Looking at her from adult eyes, he'd realized that Emma was a beautiful, desirable woman. He could hardly bear to touch her, because the friendly pats and hugs she expected were not what he wanted to give. He wanted to *touch* her. He wanted to put his palms against her arms, run them slowly down to her wrists, then back up again. He wanted to put his fingers lightly on her neck, trailing them up to her face, and across her lips. He wanted to touch her shoulders then trail his fingers over her collar bone . . .

Matt pushed himself up from the chair and walked into the bathroom. He ran the cold water tap, plunging his hands beneath the stream of water and splashing his face. Then he rubbed his face vigorously with the towel to dry it, shaking his head afterward like Poki shedding water.

He had to get thoughts of Emma out of his mind. Thoughts like those . . .

"Matt!"

Emma's excited voice called from the back of the house.

Matt closed his eyes for a moment, praying for peace of mind, then headed for the kitchen. He recalled Sonia saying earlier in the day that Emma had worn her green dress to work. He remembered her green dress. She'd worn it to church on Christmas. Emma thought it demure and elegant, but it was the kind of dress that was hard for a man to forget. Emerald green and made from some shiny stuff that seemed to cling to all her curves, the dress highlighted her shapely figure while hiding it behind long tapered sleeves, a high neck, and a calf-length skirt.

When he arrived in the kitchen, Emma was already there, and still wearing that wonderful dress. Poki lay expectantly before the cupboard that contained his food, but Matt knew he'd greeted Emma. Long golden hairs clung to the left side of her skirt. Even from across the room, he could smell the *maile*, the strong spicy scent wafting over on the gentle breeze blowing through the open windows. Emma looked so beautiful, in her emerald dress with the *maile* and crown flower lei he'd sent draped around her neck. He felt his breath catch in his throat.

"Emma." Matt smiled. "You look terrific."

It was an effort to appear casual, but he thought he achieved the proper mix of friendship and admiration.

Emma crossed the kitchen in less than a minute, sliding precipitously on the shiny linoleum in her hose-clad feet. Matt had to reach out to steady her before she crashed into him.

The smile left his face. The soft feel of her, her nearness, was almost his undoing. The urge to crush her to him and press his lips to hers was well nigh irresistible. It would be so easy to take his hands from her arms, to move them to her back and press her close. The *maile* lei squeezed between their bodies would overwhelm them with its heady scent.

The sound of Emma's laughter returned him to his senses.

"What do you think of my latest gift?" she asked, as she regained her footing. She reached for the strands of *maile*, lifting them to her nose for a deep sniff. Happiness radiated from her.

"Beautiful." He fingered a glossy leaf from the end of the strand. "Still no clues to the identity of the secret admirer?"

Emma sighed. She pulled out a chair and plopped into it. "Not a one." She rested her elbows on the table and set her chin on them, looking up at him. "The latest at work is that it must be one of the *paniolos* who comes in to cash checks."

"A cowboy?" Matt didn't have to pretend disbelief. The idea was ludicrous.

Emma shrugged, pushing some flyaway strands of hair away from her face. "Corinne likes that idea. She thinks it would be romantic to have a boyfriend who's a cowboy."

"She's young."

Emma straightened, unconsciously lifting her lei toward her nose. "Cowboys are good fantasy figures for relationships. There are lots of them in romance novels."

Matt's reaction was somewhat of a grunt. He had friends who were *paniolos*, and he didn't want any of them around Emma. One of them might be okay for Corinne, but Emma deserved more than some horse-crazy cowboy.

"If she smelled one of those cowboys when he came in from a day's work, she'd change her mind pretty quick."

Emma laughed. "You're just too practical, Matt. When we were kids and played cowboys you didn't think of stuff like that. You need to get back some of that imagination you had as a child."

Matt stared at Emma as if she was crazy. He made

his living creating games, and she thought he had no imagination?

Apparently, Emma realized what she'd just implied.

"Oh. Not that you don't have an imagination. It's just that . . ."

Matt stopped her. "It's okay. I know what you meant." But he wished he didn't. A change of subject was definitely in order.

"Look, you're all dressed up, looking terrific—what do you say we go somewhere for dinner?"

Emma smiled at him, delighted at the invitation. Then she frowned. "I don't know. Mom has dinner almost ready."

"She can come too. Go tell her to put it all in the refrigerator for tomorrow, and come join us. We'll go to one of the resorts and get a table overlooking the ocean."

Emma grinned, flashing her dimples. "I'll go tell her."

Emma started toward the door, walking at a sedate pace after her earlier mishap. As her hand touched the doorknob, she stopped and looked back. Her expression was serious.

"Matt."

She was trying to make her voice sound casual, but Matt knew her too well to be fooled. She had something serious on her mind.

"Have you ever thought about getting married?"

Matt's heart leapt in his chest. Of course he thought

of it. Every day. He'd wanted to give her a ring last Christmas, but he'd suspected she wasn't ready. The surprise gift at Valentine's Day had been a test of sorts. And she had, in effect, failed it. He never suspected it would take her so long to figure out who sent the original bouquet. And now he'd sent two more. He knew there were many people in the community who had suggested he was the one sending the gifts, but Emma dismissed them every time. She insisted she knew him too well for him to surprise her that way. Was she changing her mind?

"I would like to get married," he said carefully.

"Oh."

Her reply was so soft he barely heard it.

She stared at him for another moment, then opened the door and walked outside. She closed the door silently behind her. He could hear her stepping into her shoes, heard the click of her heels on the concrete of the lanai as she walked away.

She'd had no comment to make on his statement that he would like to marry. So she hadn't put him together with the gifts yet. So why was she asking a question like that?

When would Emma see that they were perfect for each other?

Matt struck his fist hard into the countertop, then grabbed it quickly with his other hand and held it close to his body. Darn, but that hurt. Beside him, Poki whined, his head nudging Matt's arm.

"I know, boy," he said. "I hurt myself and it's my own fault." He rubbed his hand over the furry head and was rewarded by a worshipful look. "Come on, I'll give you your dinner, but you'll have to spend the evening alone. I'm going to show Emma how romantic I am. Even if it kills me."

Although both Emma and Matt tried to persuade her, Sonia refused to go to dinner with the two young people.

"You two don't need an old lady along. You go on and have a nice romantic evening."

Matt could still hear Emma's reply.

"Don't be silly Mom. It's just Matt and me."

She'd said more, but those words were imprinted on his brain. "Just Matt and me." It was obvious that she still hadn't made the connection. It made her question about marriage all the more curious.

And on the drive to the resort, she'd done little more than speculate on the *paniolo* theory.

That was going to change right now, Matt decided as the hostess guided them to a choice table on the terrace outside the restaurant. A light breeze ruffled Emma's hair as they settled down with the menus. A busboy appeared to fill their water glasses, and a waiter soon followed. They both ordered the fish fillet and Matt selected a bottle of chardonnay after a brief conference with the waiter.

Emma waited for the waiter to leave before turning to Matt, her eyes wide.

"Matt, what are you doing? Do you know how much this meal is going to cost? Even without wine?" The timbre of her voice rose higher and higher with each question even though she worked to keep the pitch low. She'd seen the respect in the waiter's eyes when Matt requested that particular wine. It probably meant a hefty price tag. "Iced tea is fine," she insisted. "I love iced tea. Did you know that in places like this they put in a pineapple spear or a stick of sugar cane?"

Matt had to smile. Did Emma think he couldn't afford the meal? Could she really have no idea about how much money he made on his computer work and games?

"Don't worry, Emma. I can afford to buy you dinner. With wine." He sipped his water, but he couldn't hide his grin. "Besides, I already ordered it. And I think it's here," he added, as a server approached their table, wine bottle in hand.

He'd apparently set the proper tone, for Emma didn't comment again on the price of the dinner or her love of iced tea. And she didn't return to the secret admirer topic for the rest of the evening either.

They lingered over coffee and chocolate macadamia pie, laughing about the kind of everyday things they had always found to talk about. And all the while, Matt hoped that Emma was noting the romantic aspects of the evening. The terrace was unlit except for the light that flowed through the wall of glass that separated them from the inside of the restaurant. The result was a romantic glow enhanced by the candle that fluttered on their table, protected from the ocean breeze by a hurricane cover. Even the moon was co-operating with him, appearing while they ate to shine down on the ocean and the strip of pristine beach down below. A live trio played classic Hawaiian tunes. The guitar and ukulele lent a particularly romantic note to the lovely melodies.

After the meal, Matt guided Emma down the steep path leading to the beach. The water rolled across the sand with a soothing murmur. Matt wanted to walk out to the edge of the surf, but Emma balked after a few steps.

"I can't, Matt," she protested with a laugh. "My heels are sinking, and the sand is getting into my shoes."

Laughing himself, Matt scooped her up into his arms. The scent of the *maile* was overpowering as he carried her, laughing and squealing her protests, out to the edge of the water. He'd never smell *maile* again without thinking of Emma and recalling this wonderful night spent in her company.

Matt wanted to kiss her. The night, the setting, everything was absolutely perfect. Except that Emma still thought of him as the platonic friend from her youth.

In fact, she squealed loudly as he reached the edge of the water.

"Matt Correa, if you drop me in the water I'll never speak to you again."

He couldn't resist that straight line.

"Is that a promise?"

She met his grin with an indignant grunt, but they soon forgot all about the imagined threat. Their eyes met, and everything stood still for a long special moment. The silver moonlight cast its rays over them, over the palm trees, the golden sand, and the rippling water. The heady scent of the *maile* mixed with the aroma of the sea, forming a unique perfume. Their heads moved closer. Matt wanted to kiss her, knew she wanted it too. But he also knew that if he succumbed, he could never again accept their relationship as it had been. And he didn't think Emma was ready for that.

It took all his self-control, but he resisted his impulse and carried her back to harder ground.

Emma was quiet as they drove back to Malino. She sat with her head against the headrest, her eyes beginning to droop. But she straightened at Matt's words, becoming instantly alert.

"I have a favor to ask."

Her answer came with no hesitation. "Sure, Matt. You know I'm always there for you."

He had to smile. "Don't you want to hear what it is first?"

"Well, sure." She shrugged. "But I'm sure it will be okay."

Matt laughed. Her confidence in him made him feel better. "A company I do business with is having a convention here next week. They have over a hundred people flying in. I'll be attending meetings there during the day—for a couple of days. But I was hoping you'd be my guest at the banquet on Saturday evening. It's for the conference attendees and their wives," he added. "A lot of them are bringing their families because of it being in Hawaii."

"Of course I'll go with you, Matt. You just let me know what I should wear and what time to be ready." She flashed a brilliant smile toward him before settling back against the headrest once more.

Chapter Nine

Emma looked forward to her "date" with Matt, but she didn't fret over it as she had over her "secret admirer" dates. Matt had informed her of the time and place and suggested she wear her nicest muumuu. She'd marked it on her calendar and pushed it to the back of her mind. She still had other things she was concentrating on.

At work, the main topic of non-bank related conversation continued to be the identity of the secret admirer. The many *paniolos* who came into the branch were discussed, their appearances and personal relationships dissected.

It continued to amaze Emma how much even Nishiko and Sandy were interested in these discussions. Being happily married in Nishiko's case, and being turned off men in Sandy's, did little to diminish their interest in discovering the identity of the man they all agreed was the height of romanticism. The secret gifts titillated everyone's imagination.

A week after the *maile* lei arrived, Emma and Kim were setting up side by side when Kim brought up the subject of Emma's weekend date.

"So, what are you wearing to Matt's shindig?"

Emma shrugged. "I haven't given it too much thought. He said my nicest muumuu. I might wear the red one I wore to work on Valentine's Day."

"Is that your best one?"

"Well . . ." Emma hesitated. "Maybe not. But it is one of my newest ones and it's my favorite. I have a white one I got on sale at Liberty House in Honolulu." She sighed, remembering that time. Only two years ago, but seemingly a lifetime away. It had been a time of few responsibilities and fewer problems.

"My junior year, I went to an Aloha Week *Holuku* Ball. I found a fabulous white muumuu, with the little train." Her voice rose at the end of the sentence, seeming to ask Kim if she knew the style she meant.

Kim nodded eagerly. "Oh, I love those. I used to have one like it back when I danced hula. Mine was light pink." She sighed. "I wouldn't be able to get into it now."

"I fell in love with this white one," Emma continued. "I ended up getting it even though it was more than I wanted to spend—even on sale. And the white isn't really practical. But it was such a great dress and it fit like it was made for me."

"You, of all people, know you can't always be practical," Kim told her.

Emma looked startled. She turned her attention from the arrangement of her drawer. "What do you mean?" Her eyes met Kim's. "You don't think I'm practical?"

"I'm not insulting you or anything," Kim assured her. "But you have to admit you're not very practical. With your romantic ideas and all. You're pining after some imaginary secret admirer, after all, when you have that hunky Matt right next door. And taking you out to resorts, for goodness sake. Talk about a romantic evening."

Emma stopped what she was doing and stared at her friend. "Hunky Matt?"

Kim blushed but didn't back down. "Haven't you ever looked at him? He's awfully good looking, Emma. I've never understood how you can go on calling him your best friend and not want to be anything more than that."

Emma straightened the stacks of bills in her drawer, then did it all over again. She was so distracted, she didn't even notice the repetition.

She'd been working side by side with Kim for months now, almost a year straight, not including the summers while she was in college. And she'd never realized that Kim thought of Matt as anything more than her friend's friend. And now here she was calling him a hunk and sounding as though she'd like to date him herself. Imagine!

What else had she been missing? Did she have blinders on when it came to relationships? After all, she'd thought Sandy and her husband were the ideal couple. She used to watch them with envy the summer before her senior year in college. Sandy was pregnant that summer, and Joe seemed to dance attendance on her. Then, not a year after Jillian was born, they were divorcing, fighting bitterly over everything from the bedroom furniture to the family dog.

As she arranged the bills carefully in her cash drawer, Emma called up a mental picture of Matt. Her friend. Her pal.

Kim was right. Matt *was* handsome. Tall, lean. He made an effort to jog or bike every day because of his sedentary job. The result was a deeply tanned, athletic body. His features reflected his Portuguese heritage, except for his eyes, whose almond shape broadcast an Asian ancestor. His hair was dark and thick and curly and already showed a scattering of gray at the tender age of twenty-five.

She recalled how he'd looked during their dinner at the resort, wearing one of his best Aloha shirts, his hair nicely combed. He'd been entertaining and attentive. In fact, he'd been all that a date should be.

Kim was right again. It had been a romantic evening. How was it she hadn't seen it until now?

But she *was* seeing it now—Matt's shadowed face

across the candlelit table. The dim light showing off his chiseled features. His cute nose that had been broken once when he fell off a horse and so was slightly crooked. His kissable lips . . .

Emma's last thought caught her unawares. Kissable lips? She and Matt had never kissed! Unless you counted quick friendly pecks given in the name of friendship. And usually on the cheek! So where had that idea come from?

She pushed aside memories of being held in his arms, of the silvery moonlight, of the soothing sound of waves washing upon the sandy beach. Of meeting his eyes and watching his lips.

Then she remembered her mother's suggestion that Matt was just her type. Tall, athletic, dark-haired. An intelligent and focused man, a man with an established career.

Well, she wasn't certain about his job. Matt was certainly intelligent and he spent a lot of time at his computer, but she didn't really understand what it was he did there. He never seemed to worry about money though, so he must be doing okay.

Earning power was an important consideration. She wanted to have children one day, and she would love to spend those first years at home raising them. It wasn't as high on her scale as other more personal characteristics, like a gentle, caring nature, but she didn't plan to support her husband either.

Startled at this last thought, Emma quickly turned

her mind away from Matt and away from marriage, asking Kim what she planned to do tomorrow on their Prince Kuhio holiday. Everyone at the bank was looking forward to having a day off work.

But for the rest of the morning, Emma was disturbed by troubled thoughts of Matt and her relationship to him. She remembered recent instances when she'd noticed his cologne, or the heat of his body; the texture of his muscled arm. She remembered the feeling of devastation that had overwhelmed her when her mother mentioned that Matt would be getting married one of these days. The feeling of emptiness when Matt had confirmed this.

So although she summoned up a smile for Mr. Jardine when he approached her window, he took a hard look at her and asked what was wrong.

"Nothing, Mr. Jardine. I've just been doing some thinking."

"Ahh." His eyes twinkled at her. "That can be hard work."

He handed over the deposit slip he'd made out along with a small check.

"I suppose you're still worrying over that secret admirer of yours."

Emma's smile was livelier now, her voice teasing. "Are you sure it isn't you?" She inserted the deposit slip into the machine, following it with the receipt for the customer.

"Well, you never know."

He winked at her and she laughed as she handed him his receipt.

"You know, most times the solution to problems like these is right there under your nose." He tucked the receipt into his wallet and put the wallet safely away in his side pants pocket. "I know all about problem solving, you know."

"Yes, sir, I do know." Mr. Jardine had been a police officer for many, many years. He still enjoyed a reputation as one of the best detectives in the county. Everyone in town was aware of that.

"You've probably known that admirer of yours for years. One of these days it will just come to you who it is." He emphasized his point by stabbing the air in front of her with his index finger. "You just see if I'm not right."

With a firm nod, the old man moved away from her window, stopping on his way out to greet Sandy, seated at her desk.

"I sure hope so," Emma murmured after him.

But deep inside she was remembering all the people who had already told her who they thought the man was. She'd dismissed out of hand the suggestions that Matt was the secret admirer. Was it time to reconsider? For his name had occurred more than any other by those guessing the identity of her mysterious admirer.

With only half her mind occupied helping the rest of the day's customers, Emma used the other half of her brain to run through the activities of the last few weeks. It was easy to recall the gifts and their arrivals at the bank. But more important, it was equally simple to remember all the recent instances when she'd felt discomfited by Matt's presence. And their lovely evening having dinner in the moonlight, overlooking the ocean.

She surprised her Aunty Joy by laughing out loud as the older woman approached the teller window. Her aunt gave her a strange look and she quickly apologized. But she'd been comparing her date with Lance to that wonderful dinner in the moonlight, the soothing cadence of the waves in the background. The way Matt had carried her over the sand because of her high heels contrasted sharply with her weary walk through the rain with Lance. Aunty Joy would have been delighted to hear it. She was one of Matt's staunchest supporters. But Emma was still working things out. She wasn't ready to share the delicious new ideas dancing through her head. Especially with gossipy relatives.

When she finally said goodbye to Aunty Joy, she gazed unseeingly at the wide glass doors at the front of the bank.

So maybe Matt was romantic after all. But did it necessarily follow that he had sent the secret admirer gifts?

The tinkling strains of "Memories" began to play softly in her head. He *had* chosen an unbelievably lovely gift for her birthday. A sweetly romantic gift that recalled her surprise roses. If she lived to be a hundred, the porcelain music box would remain one of her most special possessions.

Emma's swiftly moving thoughts were managing to push her into an agitated state over her upcoming "date" with Matt. With only a few days left to prepare, and her newfound suspicions that Matt might indeed be the secret admirer, she began to worry about whether the red muumuu would be right and what she should do with her fly-away hair. Should she cancel their usual Saturday morning tennis match? She'd get all hot and sweaty, and her hair would get frizzy. He'd want to go over to the Dairy Queen for sodas afterward, the way they usually did. Maybe she'd need the extra time to get ready.

Emma didn't know what to think. Or what to do. She didn't usually spend hours getting ready for a date, but Saturday was shaping up into something very special.

As they prepared for closing, Emma discussed hair styles with Kim. Corinne overheard them.

"Oh, Emma. Have you got a date with another possible secret admirer? Is it one of the *paniolos*?"

Emma, who'd decided to keep her suspicions about Matt to herself for the time being, hesitated. And Kim jumped in with an answer.

"No, she's just doing her best friend a favor. Poor girl has to attend a banquet at the Halelani Resort."

"Ohhh. I wish I could go." Corinne's voice did sound envious. "Is it a dress-up thing?"

"Hawaiian dressy," Emma replied, then wondered if the term was an oxymoron.

Corinne seemed to think so. Her brows drew together. "What's that?"

Emma and Kim laughed.

"She means a nice muumuu," Kim told Corinne.

Kim turned back to Emma. With her position between the two of them, she looked like a spectator at a tennis match. "Have you decided between the red one and the white?" she asked Emma.

Emma shook her head. She explained to Corinne about the two muumuus she had, and her dilemma over which to wear.

"If it's Matt's thing, why don't you ask him?" Corinne suggested. "You always say how you two are such great friends—not boyfriend/girlfriend friends, but best friends. That's the kind of question *I'd* ask my best friend."

Emma couldn't believe she hadn't thought of it herself.

Emma popped through the hedge as soon as she got home from work. She found Matt still at his desk, busy at the computer, Poki fast asleep at his feet. The dog's head bounced up at her entrance, quickly followed by the rest of his body.

"Am I interrupting?" She reached out to pet Poki,

who was extending his usual warm welcome to her. Poki could make anyone feel loved. Male dogs were so much easier to read than male humans, Emma thought.

Matt turned toward the door, blinking rapidly as he returned to the real world. He checked his watch. "I had no idea it was so late. So, no, you're not interrupting." He got up and stretched, raising his arms almost to the ceiling, and arching his spine first one way, then the other to remove the kinks.

Emma's mouth went dry. This time she noticed her reaction immediately, and attributed it to its proper cause: a lean, athletic male body, with well-defined muscles rippling beneath his skin. And dressed in his usual T-shirt and shorts, a lot of Matt's marvelous body was available to her hungry eyes.

Good grief! She *did* find Matt attractive. How could she not have realized what was happening?

Her eyes refused to budge from the sight of Matt doing a few more stretches. His biceps bulged as he pushed his arms out, away from his body, then pulled them back in again.

Kim was right. Matt was a hunk. And she must be the last person on the island to notice.

But now she had. Her heartbeat kicked into high gear, and heat flooded her body. Her fingers ached to reach out and touch the sun-browned skin of his arms. She knew it would be hard and warm, slightly scratchy from the dark hairs liberally sprinkled over it. His legs would be the same, long and brown and hard with muscle.

Emma swallowed, her fingers tingling from her overactive imagination, from the distraction of the toned male body before her. She pressed them instead into Poki's fur, relieved to note that Matt had stopped that provocative stretching. He stepped toward the door.

Still anchored to her original spot, Emma realized that he was now much too close to her. She could smell the musky scent of him, the faint piney remnants of his morning aftershave, mixed with the heavier odor of warm male.

Emma took a deep breath to steady herself. Big mistake. The heady intake of the mixed aromas just intensified her reactions to Matt's presence. Her heart beat faster than ever. This must be what aromatherapy was all about.

She took a step back, found her spine flush against the door frame, and was grateful for the support. It gave her a moment to compose herself before following him out of the room. Several slow, even breaths helped.

Matt walked straight over to the refrigerator and removed a cold can of beer. He watched Emma surreptitiously all the way to the kitchen. Odd was a mild term to describe the way she was behaving. She'd had the strangest look in her eyes while she'd stood in the office doorway petting Poki.

He held up the can of beer. "Want one?"

Emma didn't usually drink beer, but she'd been different the last few days. So who knew anymore?

She shook her head.

"Pepsi?"

Another small head shake.

Matt took a long pull on the beer. The cool liquid felt great sliding down his throat. When he got deep into one of his programs he would forget everything around him. He didn't even come up for food or drink. Poki would pull him out of it if Matt missed one of his mealtimes, and he was grateful to the dog for that. He'd have to eat something soon now, though, or the alcohol in the beer would go straight to his head. He'd been working nonstop since mid-morning.

"So, did you want something?"

Matt's question seemed to catch Emma by surprise. Stranger and stranger. She might be energetic and restless, but she wasn't usually scatterbrained. Emma was an intelligent woman and very intuitive about people. At least about some people, he corrected himself.

She swallowed hard, then smiled. Matt loved that smile, the one that showed off only one dimple. He almost forgot her curious behavior.

"I wanted to ask you to come over and see the muumuus I might wear for Saturday's dinner. Help me pick. Since it's your function and all." She pushed her fingers through her thick hair, moving the fly-away strands away from her face. "Mom said to tell you you should come over for dinner. Then you can look at them after."

"I'd love to. I'm starved." He finished the beer and deposited the can in the receptacle under the sink. "Shall I come over now?"

"Sure. Do you need help feeding Poki?"

Matt had her replace Poki's water in the bowl out on the lanai, while he filled another bowl with food.

"He'll like being out here while I'm over at your place," he told Emma, as they finally headed through the gap in the hedge. It was a path they had trod throughout the years, first holding tightly to their mothers' hands, later, running through headlong. In adulthood, they still used the path, though their progress through it was more sedate.

Emma walked slowly. It was unlike her, Matt thought. A high-energy person, she usually strode ahead, a bounce to her step. Today, unusually, he had to slow his normal pace to allow for her smaller tread. It was something he was used to doing to accommodate other women. But he'd never had to pander to Emma in the same way.

Sonia greeted Matt with enthusiasm. Her cheeks were flushed from the heat of the stove as she checked something in a deep pan.

"Hmm, that sure smells good." Matt moved closer to the stove, sniffing appreciatively.

"Pork chops," she told him. "It'll all be ready in a

few minutes. I'm just waiting for the cornbread to finish."

"Hmm, cornbread too. I just might ask you to marry me, Mrs. Lindsey."

Sonia laughed at his silly compliment. But he could see that she was tickled by his mock proposal. Emma, however, looked startled.

"Let me help set the table," he suggested, taking the plates she had just removed from the cupboard out of her hands.

Emma readily released them, moving toward the drawer where the flatware was kept. She continued to be silent and distracted, so it gave him some time to observe her and try to determine why she was behaving in such an unusual manner.

But the minutes spent setting the table didn't help. Neither did the hour or so they spent at the table, eating Sonia's delicious dinner. He did see Sonia glance at Emma a few times, a curious look in her dark eyes. So she'd noticed it too.

As Matt passed the applesauce to Emma, he asked what she had planned for her holiday.

"Nothing special. Why?"

Matt noticed that her eyes looked less abstracted. Did she know he was working up to an invitation? Because if so he'd say she was interested.

"My cousin Kaulani teaches *keiki* hula," he began. "You remember, she started after her daughter was born? Well, Pua's three now and she's going to be in her first public show."

Emma and Sonia both exclaimed over this news.

"Is it tomorrow?" Emma asked.

Matt nodded. "It'll be at Kuhio Plaza in Hilo. They're having shows in the mall area all day, in honor of Prince Kuhio Day. Would you like to go?"

"Yes." Then she groaned. "What time? I was hoping to sleep in tomorrow."

Matt and Sonia both laughed.

"Don't worry," Matt told her. "They're not on till eleven-thirty. We can leave at ten, so you'll be able to sleep till nine or nine-thirty, depending on how much time you need to get dressed."

He proceeded to invite Sonia, who declined, pleading previous plans. He winked at her, a little signal Emma missed, then began telling them about the last time he'd seen Pua. Emma seemed less distracted, and they lingered over the rest of the meal. So it was getting late when they finally sat down in the living room, ready for Emma's mini-fashion show.

Sonia turned on the television while Emma disappeared into the bedroom to change into her first muumuu. Then she frowned over at Matt. She kept her voice low so that Emma wouldn't hear it over the sound of a sitcom on the television. "What's eating at Emma?"

Matt shrugged. He pitched his voice low as well. "I don't know. I thought she was acting strange though.

I think she's got something on her mind, but she hasn't given me a clue as to what it is."

Before they could say any more, Emma appeared in the doorway, looking more like the old Emma. She pranced through the room in her red muumuu, the wide skirt flaring around her legs as she moved. The V-neck allowed a glimpse of her golden skin and the elbow-length sleeves flattered her slim arms. He couldn't see her trim waist or long legs, but he knew they were there, hidden beneath the yards of fabric. He found the thought entrancing. Those Victorians may have known what they were doing, covering the female figure so thoroughly. Imagining what was underneath could be even more titillating than actually seeing everything a woman had to offer.

"You look lovely, dear," Sonia exclaimed. "Just like a model," she added, as Emma twirled prettily at the end of the room and started back.

"Nice," Matt agreed. Suddenly, he seemed to be having trouble speaking and had to clear his throat. More than nice. He wanted to hold her in his arms and make her melt at his touch. He'd start by kissing that shadowy spot just visible at the end of the V neckline.

Matt pulled his thoughts back to the Lindseys' living room. He had to get them off Emma and her neckline. That way led to disaster.

His gaze settled on an arrangement of fresh flowers displayed on a table in front of the window. A shallow black vase held two anthuriums, a bird of paradise, and a king protea. It was a spare but attractive grouping.

"Nice flower arrangement," he commented, as Emma disappeared down the hall to change.

If Sonia was surprised at the sudden pronouncement, she didn't show it.

"Thank you. I enjoy having fresh flowers in the house. Emma likes it too. She always has a bouquet in her bedroom."

Matt didn't want to think about Emma's bedroom. The bedroom where, right this minute, Emma was removing that loose red garment. What did she wear underneath something like that? Practical cotton? Or sexy lace?

With an effort he pulled his head together for the second time in five minutes. He was supposed to keep his thoughts centered on something neutral, he reminded himself.

But as he searched for such a topic, Emma returned. Every thought, neutral or otherwise, flew from his mind—except how beautiful Emma looked.

She wore a white muumuu, and she'd pulled her hair loosely atop her head, fastening it with a large hair clip. Numerous tendrils fell from this confinement, dripping over her ears and down her neck, reaching past the small white ruffle that encircled it. The muumuu was long and fitted, not tight, but conforming to the shape of her body. It flowed over her breasts and her hips, flaring out in a wide ruffle around her feet where it dipped toward the back, dragging along the floor behind her. White dress heels peeped out from beneath the hem with each step.

Matt released his breath in a loud swoosh. "You look great!"

Sonia laughed. "I guess that's the one then." Her eyes traveled over Emma, the love there shining through. "You do look terrific, honey. That dress is pretty enough for a bride."

Matt had been thinking the same thing. He could see it now: Emma in that lovely white dress, *maile* vines around her neck, entwined with long strings of *pikake*. White phaelenopsis in her hair. The vision was so real he thought he could smell the *maile* and *pikake*.

Emma glided by him and he realized it was just her usual gardenia scent he was smelling. Mesmerized by the sight of her, he hoped she would keep this dress for their wedding. However, since she still hadn't figured out that he was her secret admirer, there wasn't much chance she'd be willing to accept a proposal from him tonight.

"But do you think it's too dressy?" Emma looked uncertain as she glanced from her mother to Matt. "I haven't worn this since the Aloha Week *Holoku* Ball at school a couple of years ago. I'd forgotten just how formal it is."

Sonia frowned. "It is dressy, no doubt about that. What do you think, Matt? It's your party."

Matt considered. “I love the way you look in that, Emma. But I think you’re both right.” He shook his head, frowning. “I was told this would be the big end-of-conference event, and that they were encouraging the guests to wear what they called ‘dressy Hawaiian’ clothes. But I have a feeling that mainland people will think of ‘dressy Hawaiian’ as muumuus and Aloha shirts as opposed to pareaus and T-shirts.”

“Okay,” Emma said with a nod. “You’re probably right. The red one it is.”

Matt agreed, but he sure hated to see her remove that white dress. He hoped she put it away carefully, because soon he was going to propose. And he’d just seen what he hoped would be her wedding gown.

Chapter Ten

"Oh, Matt, Pua is the cutest thing I've ever seen. Those little girls in their grass skirts and plumeria leis . . ." Emma's voice trailed off. She knew Matt would understand that the little dancers were just too precious to describe with mere words.

They had watched his cousin's performance, clapping enthusiastically with the rest of the spectators at the charming little girls doing their simple hulas. They'd spent time with Pua and her mother afterward, too, walking over to the food court for lunch. Pua had been almost too excited to eat, bouncing up and down in her seat, nibbling at her food and talking non-stop. Emma had eaten her own food quietly, watching Matt interact with the little girl. He was wonderful with her, and knowledgeable about things that interested her.

Emma realized with a start that she herself had no idea what three-year-olds liked to do.

They were back in the car now, driving through downtown Hilo and heading for the highway.

"They were something, weren't they?" Matt said. "I want to have kids of my own," he went on. "They can be difficult, but I think they give more pleasure than trouble, don't you?"

Startled at the direction the conversation had taken, Emma stuttered over her answer. "Oh, ah . . . I, ah . . . agree. My nieces can be a pain, but most of the time they're very sweet and loving."

Emma stared out the window as she replied, afraid to look toward Matt. She didn't want him to see how painful she found it, facing the thought of him having children with some stranger.

"Do you want to have children, Emma?"

"Yes, I do."

Emma didn't say anything more, and neither did Matt. It was obvious to her that something subtle was changing between them. This was the kind of question they would often debate—deep, personal questions that they didn't discuss with others except abstractly. But suddenly it felt awkward to admit to Matt that she wanted children. The question of who would father them seemed to float in the air between them, unspoken but heavy with meaning.

Emma, dreaming of toddlers with Matt's curly dark

hair—came out of her reverie only when Matt turned the car off the main road:

"Matt, where are you going?"

Matt smiled. "We have the day off, so I thought we'd take a little side trip."

Emma stared out the car window at the fields where wild cane grew. This whole area had been planted with sugar cane at one time and although the plantations no longer existed, the abandoned fields were still filled with stalks of the grass-like plants. "Where are we going?"

Matt replied with a question of his own. "How long has it been since you saw Akaka Falls?"

Emma sighed with pleasure. It had been years and years. The steep waterfall was one of the prettiest on the island, viewed after a walk through the rain forest. There were masses of blooming flowers and little wooden bridges over clear creeks flowing with cold mountain water. It was quite a romantic place.

"It's been forever," she finally said.

Matt's voice turned cautious. "And did you want to see it again?"

"Oh, yes." Her voice was as eager as her answer.

The walk to the falls was everything Matt had hoped. Emma exclaimed over the banks of varicolored impatiens, at the thick stands of bamboo. A brief stumble on the lava rock steps allowed Matt to loop his arm around the back of Emma's waist to offer her his support. As they drew closer and closer to the viewing area, he drew closer and closer to Emma.

Oblivious of the natural beauty around them, Matt was aware of nothing but the woman beside him. Her soft, warm body imprinted itself against his long hard one. Her wild hair brushed his cheek, sending prickly tingles through his skin. Her light gardenia fragrance invaded his pores.

He didn't return to reality until Emma came to a stop.

"Ohhh."

The long drawn-out breath was Emma's response to the sight of the twin falls, suddenly there before them after their long walk.

Matt's arms moved to her shoulders. "Beautiful, isn't it?" he asked. But his eyes were on Emma's face, not the deep green gorge or the twin waterfalls.

"It is." Emma's voice was hushed.

Matt squeezed her against his side. Pouring from the green-coated walls of a deep gorge, the water of Akaka Falls plunged hundreds of feet to the pool below. The water mist around the base hid the lower area entirely. And to the right, Kahuna Falls, not as tall but equally lovely. Together, they were a sight of breathtaking natural beauty.

Matt and Emma watched in silence, enjoying the natural wonder before them. Then Emma turned. She'd meant to place a kiss on Matt's cheek, her usual impulsive gesture of thanks when he did something special for her. But Matt anticipated the action and angled his head, so that her lips landed on his.

Emma stilled. Matt's lips beneath hers were soft and cool, slightly damp from the "liquid sunshine" of the rain forest. Her eyelids drooped as she increased the pressure of her lips against his. She already felt a languid peace from their long walk, and the warmth of his contact. Somehow, to give him a "real" kiss now seemed just right.

Matt tightened his arm around her. He drew her toward him until they stood chest to chest, and his other arm joined the first to enclose her in a warm embrace. He pulled her closer still. She fit so perfectly against him. He wanted to lose himself in the kiss, wanted her to lose her control as well. If she did, she might finally admit her feelings for him, feelings he knew existed. And he could propose right here in this seductive location.

And then a magical thing happened. They heard bells! Faint, intermittent, but nevertheless clear. A bell was tinkling, lightly, far away, but drawing ever closer.

Matt and Emma pulled apart and stared at each other in wonder. They were still standing there, side by side, Matt's arm draped loosely around Emma's shoulders, when a group of chattering tourists arrived. Leading the way was a young couple, the father holding a tiny girl in his arms. She was agitating to be put down, kicking her legs wildly as she repeated the words, "down, down."

Emma, still reeling from Matt's proximity during their walk in and from the devastating kiss, stared at the girl's shoes. She wore little saddle shoes; tied into the laces were tiny jingle bells.

Emma began to laugh. She'd always said she wanted to hear bells when she kissed a man. And now she had.

"So what did you do on your day off?"

Kim and Emma were back in their usual places on Thursday morning, getting ready for the day's business. Kim's question fell into the unusual silence that lay around Emma. But it pulled a quick smile from her.

"Oh, Kim, it was wonderful." Emma stopped checking her stacks of forms and looked up. "Matt took me to a *keiki* hula show in Hilo. His cousin teaches a group of young kids."

Kim looked into space for a moment, then smiled. "Kaulani."

Emma laughed. "How did you know?"

Kim shrugged. "She went to school with my sister. So how was the show?"

"It was terrific! Kaulani's three-year-old daughter, Pua, was in it. She is the sweetest thing!" She sighed. "Makes me wish I had kids of my own."

Sandy rushed into the bank just as Emma finished speaking.

"Sorry I'm late. Jillian threw up all night and I had to get my mother over to watch her this morning. I'll have to go home at lunchtime to check on her, but we think it's just the flu." She collapsed into the chair behind her desk. "I don't think I slept more than a couple of hours altogether last night. I'm exhausted!"

Kim and Emma exchanged a look over the top of their windows and burst into laughter. Sandy glanced over at them, frowning.

"Sorry," Kim apologized, grinning at Sandy. "I'm really sorry Jillian is sick . . ."

"Me, too," Emma chimed in.

"But it's just that Emma was just saying how she wanted to have kids of her own." Kim couldn't suppress another chuckle. "Because they're so cute and sweet."

"Welcome to real life," Sandy deadpanned.

Because they had to open the doors then, it wasn't until a lull an hour later that Emma and Kim had another chance to talk. There were no customers and it was Emma's turn to ask Kim about her holiday. To her surprise, Kim had had a date with Lance.

"Lunch at the seafood restaurant?" Emma inquired.

"How'd you know?" Kim laughed. "And we walked along the beach afterward. I enjoyed myself. He's not as bad as you tried to make out."

Emma shrugged. "I said at the time he might not be

so bad. Except that I was expecting the secret admirer. I had high standards." And, she thought, a walk along the beach on a lovely sunny day was a far cry from a walk along the beach on a cold, windy, and rainy night.

"So no more dates on plan?"

"Not unless you count Saturday night with Matt."

Emma's voice went soft and she wondered if Kim noticed. She didn't want to tell anyone about her suspicions yet. Not even those who had presumed all along that Matt was the not-so-secretive admirer.

Kim did notice. She eyed Emma.

"Are you finally taking this date seriously?"

"I guess so." Emma thought for a moment, then nodded. "Yes, I am. He took me to Akaka Falls yesterday."

"He did?"

Mr. Jardine had walked in just in time to hear this last exchange.

"Ah, have you discovered your admirer then? Or are you still having tryouts?"

Emma and Kim both laughed.

"Tryouts? Honestly." Emma smiled at the old man as he stopped in front of her. He put a check on the counter and she reached for it automatically. "No, I was just telling Kim about going to Akaka Falls with Matt yesterday."

Mr. Jardine chuckled. "Akaka Falls. Lovely place. Lovely song." He took off his cap and put it back on, making some adjustment only he was aware of. "Matt Correa, eh? So, is he the one?"

She replied as usual. "Matt? Oh, I don't think so."

Emma wondered if they noticed that, for the first time since Matt's name was offered as candidate for secret admirer, her voice lacked conviction.

Emma was almost ready for her big "date" with Matt. She'd pampered herself earlier with a long bath, soaking in water lightly oiled and scented with her favorite gardenia fragrance. She was dressed in her red muumuu, feeling relaxed as she finished her last-minute preparations.

Now if only she could do something with her hair! She ran the brush through it once more, though there wasn't much she could do with the curly mass. She'd washed it earlier, and used a conditioner that was supposed to make it behave. Yet it spread over her shoulders and down her back past her shoulder blades in its usual uninhibited manner. Thankfully, Matt had often said that he liked the way it looked.

She cocked her head at her reflection in the mirror. Perhaps a gardenia on the side, she thought. She could pick one on the way out to the car.

She was reaching for a tube of lipstick when the front doorbell rang. Now who on earth could that be? Emma wondered. It was almost time for Matt to pick her up.

She hurried from her room, meeting Sonia in the

entry, an equally curious expression gracing her face. Most of their company came through the side door, the one that led into the kitchen. Through the glass pane inserted into the center of the front door, they could see Matt standing outside. Exchanging a look of surprise with her daughter, Sonia opened the door.

Standing behind her mother, Emma stared at Matt, a feeling almost of hunger overwhelming her. He looked good enough to eat. His dark hair had been trimmed and was neatly combed, the forward strands curling over his forehead to create a slightly rakish air. His eyes were bright and his lips were parted in a smile that hit Emma with the impact of New Year's Eve firecrackers. He wore a gold Aloha shirt with red flowers on it. To match her muumuu, Emma thought with delight.

His eyes moved from Emma to Sonia, and his brows rose at their matching looks of surprise.

"Am I early?" He looked down at his clothes. "Inappropriately dressed?"

With a laugh, Sonia pulled him into the house. "No, no. We're just surprised to see you at this door. You always come in the back." She closed the front door and turned to look at him. "And you look great. Doesn't he, Emma?"

Matt's eyes turned to Emma. "I wanted to make it seem like a real date." He laughed, though it was more wry than funny. "You can pretend it's one of your secret admirer tryout dates," he told her.

Emma didn't laugh, just smiled quietly. "Tryout" was the same term Mr. Jardine had used and she was beginning to think it the appropriate word. Should she tell him she would allow him a "tryout" date? Should this be it?

But before she could say anything, Matt held out his hand. She hadn't noticed them until now, being intrigued by how handsome he looked, but he held a spray of orchids.

"I wanted to bring you a ginger lei, but it wouldn't have been appropriate for this tonight. They might even provide leis for all the guests, I don't know." He shrugged, an echo of his words. "So I brought some flowers for your hair."

Emma took the stem of orchids with silent appreciation. They were white phaelenopsis, the beautiful pure white blossoms so often used to make a bride's bouquet.

"Oh, Matt. They're beautiful."

Today, with her thoughts tumbling around her physical reactions to Matt and whether or not he could be the secret admirer, Emma held back on her impulse to run over and kiss his cheek. The confusion caused by his nearness made her shy. The scent of his cologne made her dizzy. So she smiled at him, turned, and fled toward her room.

Matt looked after her with a curious yearning. He'd never understand women.

He heard Sonia laugh and pulled his mind away from the futile task of analyzing Emma.

"She's just going to pin them in her hair."

Sonia gestured for Matt to take a seat in the living room.

"I think it's finally coming to her," she told him quietly.

Matt stared at her. Did Sonia mean what he thought she did? Was Emma finally coming to realize that she didn't have to look too far from home to find her admirer?

He'd counted on that St. Patrick's day dinner to show Emma how romantic he could be. It had gone very well from his point of view. He'd had a wonderful evening with her. He thought she'd enjoyed it as well. But the candlelight dinner hadn't done anything to nudge her in the proper direction when it came to guessing the identity of her secret admirer. Nor had the moonlight and surf afterward.

Then there was their little visit to Akaka Falls yesterday. It had been a special time, a rare kiss. Even Emma had to be aware of that. Yet, still, she'd said nothing to him about her feelings for him or the secret admirer.

Emma returned to the room then, her heeled sandals held by their straps in one hand. All rational thought fled his mind. A light scent of gardenias floated across the room toward him at her approach, further jumbling his senses. The hem of the red muumuu fluttered over the floor as she moved, giving the impression that she floated across the carpet toward him. She had pinned the orchids into her hair on the left side of her face.

Matt blinked and looked again. The white blossoms were clustered from her forehead to her ear, nestled in the fine curly strands that flew about her head in their usual unruly style. The left side.

A wide masculine grin erupted on Matt's face. So she'd decided she was his. For tonight anyway, and he could work on the tomorrows. The mainland people at the party wouldn't know about the Polynesian tradition, but he knew. Flowers over the right ear: available. Flowers over the left ear: taken.

And most important of all, Emma knew.

"You're beautiful."

Emma ducked her head, embarrassed by the color that flooded her cheeks at his compliment. Matt often gave her compliments. She'd always asked his opinion about clothing and such, and he was always honest. Maybe that's why she was blushing this way now.

"Well, go on, you two." Sonia shooed them toward the door. "You don't want to be late."

Obediently, they moved outside. Matt stepped into the Docksiders he'd left beside the door mat, then took Emma's elbow to help steady her while she slipped on her sandals.

Emma managed to hold herself still while she slid her feet into her sandals, but it required effort. The firm pressure of Matt's hand on her arm was sending shock waves through her system. The reaction couldn't have been far different if she'd stuck her finger into an open socket. The urge to lean against his solid bulk was almost irresistible.

And he didn't let her go when she'd donned the shoes and they started toward his car. In fact, it was even worse then, for he held his hand lightly against the small of her back. She had become so sensitive to his touch that prickles of pleasure washed over her, starting in her lower back and radiating outward through her body.

She breathed a sigh of relief as she finally seated herself in the front seat of the car and Matt closed the door. She was still settling her skirts around her when he sat beside her in the driver's seat. A whiff of citrus and spice caught her unawares, making her heart trip. How was she going to manage this drive? She was closed into a small car with a large man. A man wearing the most delectable cologne on the market.

Emma touched the button that rolled down the window.

Matt was negotiating the turn onto the highway, but he noticed.

"Won't that wreck your hairdo?"

Emma laughed. Just what she needed—fresh salt-scented air, and laughter.

"Nothing can ruin my hairdo. The flowers are on the other side so the breeze won't harm them. And no matter what I do to my hair it flies around my head however it wants to. So a little fresh air won't matter."

"I love your hair." And everything else about you, Matt added to himself. He hoped he'd be able to tell her soon.

"Thanks." Emma desperately wanted to get the conversation away from such personal things. Even with the window open she could detect lingering traces of citrus and spice. "Tell me about the people I'm going to meet tonight."

Matt plunged into an explanation of the company and the convention and his business with them, then moved on to descriptions of a few of the people he'd met in the past two days.

By the time they arrived at the hotel, Emma's mind was so full of details, she completely forgot about how nervous she was.

"How could I ever have believed that Matt was not romantic?" Emma asked herself later that night as she snuggled under the covers in her bed. Well, Sunday morning actually. They had gotten back after midnight, and she was having a hard time falling asleep as her thoughts swirled around in her head.

How could she have been so blind for all these years? Kim was right. Matt was a hunk. And now she had every reason to believe he was the one sending her the secret admirer gifts. But just in case it wasn't so, she hadn't wanted to spoil the evening by suggesting it. She'd face him later. Tomorrow—or, rather today—perhaps.

Her eyes stared at the silvery moon-patterns on the wall, but she wasn't seeing them. Instead she saw Matt. Matt, her dear friend. Matt, the handsomest man she knew. And the smartest.

With a sigh of contentment, she rolled over, pulling the coverlet around her shoulders and thinking back to the party.

It had been a wonderful evening. Everyone was in a party mood after three days of meetings. And everyone knew Matt, and welcomed them. At first, Emma thought they knew him because of the recent meetings. But it turned out that many of the men were meeting him for the first time that evening. Matt was a genuine celebrity in their world!

The pleasant feeling of contentment Emma felt evaporated. She wanted to pull the covers over her head in shame as she was forced to some disconcerting conclusions about herself. She'd become a self-centered twit. It was obvious to her now. All those hours she spent with Matt. She told him everything that happened in her life, everything she cared about, everything she yearned for. But had she once bothered to ask Matt about his life? About his work? About his goals?

Because what she'd learned tonight made her realize that Matt Correa was a lot more than her neighbor and her friend. More even than the inventor of computer games. Matt was a highly respected businessman. Her Matt. And she hadn't known.

Even alone in the darkened room, Emma could feel her cheeks burning with shame. Of course she knew about the game. While she'd never been into computer games herself, she'd played TygR a few times over at Matt's. It was fun. They were both still in college when he'd come up with the concept that made the game possible, and she had heard all about it. Knew that it had been a surprising success. Matt had been both proud and happy. And of course, she'd been proud of him.

So when had she become so lost in self-pity that she stopped asking him about himself? About his work? Why hadn't she known about his continuing development of animation techniques? That was what interested the men and women at the convention, and it was obvious to her that it interested Matt a great deal as well.

Emma rolled over to the other side, pushing at her pillow to try to make it more comfortable. She gave up with a sigh. It wasn't the pillow. She was uncomfortable with who she had become.

She supposed it happened after her father died, when she'd known that she had to come home. Her mother had not asked her to do it. Neither had Malia. Emma made the decision on her own. And then she'd blamed them both. Oh, not out loud. Outwardly she'd tried to make the best of things, but internally the discontent had festered until all she could think about was her boring daily life and her unhappiness with it. More and more she'd lost herself in her books and fantasies.

She flopped over onto her back and stared at the gloomy ceiling. Daily life. It wasn't so bad really. She had the joy of working with people like Kim and Nishiko. Nishiko was a good boss, fair to her employees. And Kim had become her best friend, after Matt. And of course there were the customers. Oh, some of them could be a royal pain, but there were so many more like Mr. Jardine and Aunty Liliuokalani—nice, friendly people who took an interest in the lives of the bank employees. Even Aunty Joy could be fun to talk to. She had the family genealogy stored in her sharp mind and she could tell Emma about relations from generations back.

And there was Sonia. Emma loved her mother. She had been doubly hurt at the loss of her father, because of the way it had broken her mother's heart. But in the past ten months, she'd seen Sonia coming out of it, beginning to live again. She liked to think that her being there had played a part in Sonia's recovery.

Her parents had been very much in love for the duration of their thirty-eight-year marriage. But her father had taken such good care of his "little woman" that Sonia was barely able to manage after his death. Emma had to instruct her in the most basic of things—like balancing the checking account and seeing that all the bills were paid on time. It wasn't that her mother was stupid. But she had an artistic temperament that didn't always focus on the more practical side of life. However, she had made excellent progress in the past year and Emma was increasingly optimistic.

Early this year Sonia had brought out her paints and was spending her mornings on the beach, doing watercolors again. Sonia was a talented artist, and now that she was painting once more, Emma knew that she would be all right.

Emma sat straight up in bed as she came to a sudden realization. She wasn't unhappy in Malino. She had a good, satisfying life here. She had family and good friends, and a relaxing lifestyle. If she'd gotten one of those power jobs she'd craved, she might be jetting around the world. But she might also have been stressed to the point of poor health. She'd lost touch with many of her old classmates because they were just too busy with their jobs in Honolulu and the mainland. Too busy to take a few minutes to jot a note to her, or to make a phone call.

"I don't want to be like that."

Emma clapped her hand over her mouth as she realized that she'd said it out loud. In the deep silence of the late hour, the quietly spoken words were like a shout.

She stifled the laughter that threatened to overflow. She was happy! She *wanted* to live in quiet Malino with her mother and Matt and all the people she'd known her entire life.

With Matt. Definitely with Matt.

Emma pushed her pillow against the headboard and leaned back, pulling the coverlet up to her chin. What a fool she was! All those strange feelings she'd been having. How many times had she told herself she must be coming down with something because of disturbing reactions around Matt? When he got too close. When he took off his shirt to do yard work. The rapid heartbeat she'd feared was a medical condition was nothing more than her body telling her that she admired Matt. A lot!

Emma hugged herself. What a time to recognize those feelings for what they really were! She was in love with Matt, and probably had been for a long time. She glanced at the bedside clock. The little glowing numerals told her it was 3:23 AM. Not the time to crash through the hedge and push open Matt's kitchen door. Not the time to blurt out her newly discovered love for him.

She should have known long before this that Matt was the secret admirer. So many others had recognized the fact that he must be the one. The special gifts had revealed an intimate knowledge of Emma, of her likes and dislikes. She should have known from the start. How could anyone else have known about the yellow roses with the pink edges? Most men sent red roses on Valentine's Day. They were supposed to mean love. Only her Matt would know that the yellow ones would be even more special to her.

And then there was the birthday music box. He'd been giving her a hint—and she still hadn't gotten it!

Emma slid down between the sheets, releasing her breath in a long sigh and closing her eyes. Now that she'd worked it all out in her mind, she knew that sleep would come. There would be plenty of time to tell Matt she loved him; *after* she got a good night's sleep.

Chapter Eleven

Emma stood before the mirror staring at the wild woman gazing back at her. At three this morning, everything had seemed so simple. At three this afternoon, she wondered if she had the courage to go next door and face Matt. Frowning in despair at her unmanageable hair, she scooped it all up onto the top of her head and secured it with a large clip. Then she leaned in close, her frown growing more severe. Were those dark circles under her eyes?

"Emma, are you ready?" Sonia's voice filtered down the hall from the central part of the house.

"Ready?" Emma walked to the door and peeked out. "Ready for what?"

"You haven't forgotten?" Sonia's voice showed her exasperation.

"We're already running late. It's the first birthday luau for Keanu—you know, Mitch and Amy's little boy?"

"I did forget," Emma said, joining her mother in the kitchen. "But that's okay. I'm ready." She didn't have to tell her mother that she'd put on her favorite shorts and top so that she would feel pretty and confident when she went over to see Matt.

"Is Matt going?"

Sonia gave her a strange look.

"Of course Matt is going. We're riding with him." Sonia shook her head. "What's with you this afternoon, Emma? Too much party last night?"

She took some tissues from the box on the kitchen counter and folded them into her purse. "It's Matt's cousin, you know. Amy's mother is his first cousin. Her mother was a half-sister of Bernie's." As always when Matt's mother was mentioned, a sad look washed over Sonia's face. They had been best friends for so many years, she still missed the other woman.

But she recovered quickly and went on. "And we're related to Mitch, of course. He's a distant cousin through my father's side of the family."

Sonia continued with her short course in genealogy as she grabbed the colorfully wrapped birthday gift from the counter and pushed Emma out the door, only to be stopped by Emma's gasp of surprise.

"Oh!" The cry escaped Emma's lips before she could catch it back.

Emma had come within an inch of smashing into a wide male chest clad in a green Aloha shirt. The scent of citrus and spice crept into her nostrils. Matt's unique scent. It filled her senses and clouded her mind so that she had to reach for his arm to steady herself.

Bad mistake. Her fingers burned from the warmth of his skin. They tingled from the roughness of the hairs that covered his arm. As soon as she caught her balance, she pulled her hand back. But she could still feel him through the soft pads of her fingertips. And she felt no steadier now than she had before; her brief wobble wasn't caused by a physical imbalance, but by the sensual overload brought about by Matt's closeness.

Matt gave her a curious smile and Emma ducked her head. He must be wondering what was going on with her. She was wondering herself.

Sonia barely gave them time to greet each other, hurrying toward Matt's car. She insisted on climbing in back.

"You young people will want to visit," she insisted.

Sonia continued to chatter for the for the part of the trip, but after a few minutes declared she would lose her voice before they arrived from talking over the sounds of wind and traffic. She settled back into her seat, silent and expectant, waiting for the younger couple to speak.

Matt peeked over at Emma, easily visible in his peripheral vision. Something was wrong with her. He didn't know what, but it was obvious to him. She was acting shy, for one thing. And being shy had never been one of Emma's problems.

"Did you get enough sleep last night?" he finally asked.

"Oh, yes."

Now why would a simple question like that make her flustered?

"I'd forgotten about the luau until Mom called me, though. She was explaining how we're both related to the baby when I almost bumped into you."

"Ah. Riveting stuff."

Emma laughed. "Yeah."

"Mitch and Amy sure are happy together."

"Hmm."

Emma rested her head against the seat back. She seemed more relaxed now than when they'd started out.

"I hadn't seen Amy for a while," Emma continued. "But she stopped in at the bank a few weeks ago. She had little Keanu with her, and he's so cute. He's walking already—running, in fact. She says he's wearing her out."

Matt smiled. Amy didn't have the energy Emma had always exhibited, so her son just might be doing that. Matt watched Emma in his peripheral vision. Emma, with her high energy levels, was made to be the mother of a toddler. He could just see her, chasing a little girl, round with baby fat, brown-skinned and almond-eyed, and with the same curly fly-away hair. Their daughter . . .

The dream faded with the realization that Emma still couldn't accept him as more than a friend. He'd been so sure that after the last few days . . .

"Amy and Mitch were high school sweethearts," he said. "They practically grew up together."

At the edge of his field of vision, he saw Emma stiffen, then relax again. Good. She realized that he was debating their own relationship, arguing against her point that they were such good friends they could never be suitable lovers.

Emma stretched her legs out in front of her. And laughed. "So were Frank and Clarice."

Matt had to laugh too. The little minx. Frank and Clarice had indeed been high school sweethearts. Famous for their romance that survived four full years of high school, they married within a month of their graduation day and divorced a year later after twelve months of constant arguments. The interesting thing, and the point to Emma's remark, of course, was that since their divorce they were once again great friends.

"Point taken." Matt was willing to give her one. Besides, they had arrived at Mitch and Amy's. Time enough later to talk to Emma.

Emma all but lost hope of ever speaking to Matt alone that day. Although the party started in the early afternoon, it lasted well into the night. Copious amounts of food and drink kept the participants happy, and afterward there was the singing of "Happy Birthday" and the opening of presents. Eventually, little Keanu fell into an exhausted sleep, sprawled across his mother's lap, while the musicians continued to play around him, and voices rose in spontaneous sing-alongs.

Throughout the evening, Emma found herself watching Mitch and Amy. They had been in a class between Matt's and hers, but she did remember them from high school. They were the couple who made out in the corner of the gym at the school dances, the ones who barely moved during the slow numbers, just standing on the dance floor and shifting their weight back and forth as they held tightly to one another.

Watching them now, after three years of marriage and one child, Emma saw them exchanging those same loving looks, touching when they passed close enough. It was the corroboration she needed.

By the time they climbed into the car for the drive home, Emma felt as tired as little Keanu. But she knew that sleep would elude her as it had the night before. As it probably would until she had that talk with Matt.

So when Matt stopped in front of their house to drop off Sonia, Emma stayed in the car.

"I just want to tell Matt something, Mom," she told Sonia when questioned. "I'll be right along."

Sonia grinned. "Take your time, hon. I'll leave the light on for you."

Matt was thoughtful as he pulled the car back out into the street and into his own driveway, parking it in the carport. Emma didn't follow him out, so he walked around to open her door. More and more interesting. He didn't mind playing the gentleman, but Emma usually had little patience for such things.

Still seated in the car, staring unseeingly through the windshield, Emma seemed startled to have him standing beside her, peering in at her through the opened door. With a gasp of surprise, she scurried out, and hurried toward the house.

Matt smiled. He thought he knew what she wanted to talk about. Anyway, he sure hoped he did. And it was about time.

He continued to grin as he unlocked the front door and ushered her in. A sleepy Poki appeared, tail wagging mightily, to welcome them. Matt patted his head.

"Would you like to come back to the kitchen and have some coffee?" he asked. Then he frowned. "Or is it too late for coffee?"

Emma didn't reply. She was stroking Poki's head in response to the dog's nudge of her hand.

Matt closed the door behind them, wondering if she'd even heard him. So he tried again.

"Why don't we go into the kitchen and have some hot chocolate? That won't keep us awake later like coffee might."

This time Emma did hear him. She beamed a high-wattage smile in his direction; both dimples flashed.

"What a good idea!"

Matt thought her reaction too over-the-top for an invitation to join him in a cup of hot chocolate. So he must be right about her intentions to finally talk about their relationship. And she was putting it off as long as possible.

He smiled as he followed her into the kitchen. Poki, responding to the upbeat note in Emma's voice, pranced along beside them.

Emma ran her finger along the edge of her mug, feeling the steam rising hot against the edge of her fingertip. She and Matt had made small talk about general subjects while the milk heated, and she'd fussed over Poki. But now they were both seated at the table with full mugs of chocolate in front of them. Poki lay quietly beside them, his eyes alert to any food that might appear. Matt gazed at her expectantly, waiting to hear what she wanted to say to him; what was important enough to have her follow him home after midnight, on a night when she would have to awaken early the next morning for work.

She cleared her throat.

"Did you say something?"

Emma frowned at him. He knew very well that she hadn't said a word.

She peered into his eyes. They were sparkling with amusement. What was going on here? Did he know what she meant to say?

Still frowning, Emma took a tentative sip of the hot cocoa. There just was no easy way to approach this, so she decided to plunge in with both feet. Setting down her mug, she blurted out her question.

"Matt, are you my secret admirer?"

His grin transformed his face. He might have been handsome before, sitting there sipping from his mug, looking at her with that amused glint in his eyes. But now he was movie-star gorgeous. The rakish grin, the hair falling across his forehead . . . Yes, Kim was right. Matt was a hunk.

"I thought you'd never ask." He continued to beam at her.

Emma was so overwhelmed by her sudden appreciation of his good looks, she could hardly hold a rational thought in her mind. She shook her head in a vain attempt to clear it.

"Is that a yes?"

Matt abandoned his mug, coming to his feet and drawing her up beside him. His hands settled on her upper arms, rubbing them lightly up and down as he peered into her face.

Emma was amazed to find herself still standing before him. His hands moving along her arms made her skin tingle and her bones dissolve. She ought to be puddled at his feet right now, down there beside Poki, not staring into his dark eyes. Seeing the desire and the love there.

The love.

Her breath came out on a soft sigh. Definitely an adoring look.

"Emma. My sweet ridiculous Emma." Matt crushed her to him, his arms wrapping around her back to hold her firmly against his chest as he dropped light kisses into her hair.

Emma tried to disregard the pounding of her heart, the sweet shivers that were her body's response to his kisses.

She pushed back enough to look up at him.

"What do you mean, ridiculous?"

Matt sat on one of the kitchen chairs, pulling her down into his lap. But Emma struggled up, and took a chair of her own.

"I can't think with you that close," she told him. A nervous giggle escaped her throat, surprising and embarrassing her.

Matt laughed. Loud and long and with great appreciation.

Emma tried to look offended, but it was hard to do so with Matt being so loudly cheerful.

"And that settles it all right there," he said.

Emma allowed him to take her hand. It wasn't nearly as distracting as being in his arms. But she still felt completely in the dark. Her brows drew together. "*What* are you talking about?"

He couldn't resist another chuckle.

"I'm talking about you and me, Emma. And your foolish theory that we can't become lovers or spouses because we're such good friends. It's ridiculous. Lots of people who have known each other forever and were great friends get married. And stay married," he said quickly when he saw she was ready to interrupt. "In fact, being best friends is the best argument I can think of for a marriage between us to work."

Emma squeezed his hand. "It's taken me a long time to realize how much I care about you, Matt. And it wasn't just because I finally figured out you must be the secret admirer. It's been happening gradually over the past couple of months. I've just been more aware of you . . ."

Emma faltered, not wanting to admit to the sensual feelings she'd been having—and failed to recognize. "I thought something was wrong with me, that I was coming down with something. I just couldn't imagine us being anything more than the best of friends."

Her cheeks flushed with embarrassment as she admitted to him her naiveté. Matt loved her all the more for it. "And can you now?"

Matt reached over and brushed a strand of hair from near her eye. His gentle touch brought tears to her eyes. She blinked rapidly.

"Oh, yes. I want to be in your arms now, even though I can't even think when I'm that close to you. I love the thought of coming home to you at night and talking over our days."

"And then there are those nights . . ."

Emma blushed a deeper shade of crimson.

"And having babies with you," she said shyly. "Like little Keanu."

"I can't think of anything I'd like more. Except maybe a little girl who looks just like you."

"And, don't worry, Matt. I'll keep working at the bank. Mom will probably babysit for free, so you won't have to worry about the expense."

Matt took his hands from her and put them on her upper arms, holding her at arm's length so he could look her straight in the eyes. "Emma. What are you talking about?"

Emma frowned. "I'm talking about how we'll live after we're married. I sure didn't expect you to get all macho about me working, Matt. I don't care if you don't make a lot of money. As long as you like what you're doing . . ."

She broke off when Matt began to laugh. His hands fell from Emma's arms, and his head bowed to his knees. He laughed until tears began to gather in the corners of his eyes.

Emma sat where she was. Her eyes narrowed, her mouth opened, then closed. Unusual as it was, she couldn't think of a thing to say. What had gotten into Matt?

Matt finally got control of himself. He sat back up, wiped the corner of his right eye, and took both of Emma's hands in his. Still smiling, he shook his head.

"Emma . . . I knew you were a little vague about what exactly it is that I do. But I had no idea you were worried about the financial state of my business. Emma, MJC Corporation is worth over five hundred million dollars. And I own all the shares."

His grin widened as Emma's eyes did.

"But I can't tell you how happy it makes me to know that you would marry me even if I *was* just a poor hacker working away at a dream."

"Five *hundred* . . . ?" Emma's voice rose so high it was barely audible. "I can stay at home when we have a baby?"

Matt nodded. "Even before if you want to." He pulled her to her feet, his arms snaking around her. His voice lowered. "Our baby. I love the sound of that."

Emma's arms tightened around him. "So do I."

Matt's head lowered and his lips brushed her skin, but she felt it all the way to her heart.

As one, they rose to their feet, reaching for one another. Matt's lips closed over Emma's.

It was quite late when she finally crossed the hedge and turned off that light Sonia had left on for her.

Chapter Twelve

"Honestly, Emma," Kim said, during one of the lulls in business the next morning. "That must have been some party yesterday. You've got dark circles under your eyes, yet you've been so happy all morning you're beginning to make me sick."

"I like it," Nishiko commented. "It makes me happy to have people around me in such good spirits."

"Oh, my." Corinne's voice, heavy with envy, broke through their conversation. "Look at what's coming. And it's not a holiday and you already had your birthday."

All heads turned toward the door. Mr. Jardine stood there, holding the glass door open for Luana Young. Luana was trying hard to hide her triumph, but her grin refused to disappear.

"More flowers from that secret admirer, Ms. Lindsey," Mr. Jardine announced. "Did you figure out who it is yet?"

There being no other customers in the bank besides the old man, everyone gathered around Emma's window. Luana handed over the bouquet. Roses again, the same yellow long-stems with the pink blushed tips that had arrived on Valentine's Day, almost two months ago. This time they were in a white vase with a cherub at the front.

"Sign here."

Luana handed her the clipboard and pen, smiling wide enough to give serious competition to Bozo the Clown.

Kim eyed her suspiciously. "What's with you today, Luana? You look like a cat that just ate her owner's favorite canary."

"Oh!" Corinne startled them all with her squeal of delight. "I'll bet she knows! She knows who it is!" Corinne's whole body bounced in excitement. "He must have ordered them in person this time! Oh, quick, Emma. Open the card."

But Emma's smile mirrored Luana's. And she refused to be rushed.

"They're beautiful, Luana."

She held the vase in her hands, leaning over to sniff the delicate scent of the rosebuds. She allowed the soft petals to trail across her cheek, reveling in the feel of it—almost as wonderful as the gentle touch of Matt's fingers across her cheek.

The others all watched her, amazed at her sedate reaction.

"Well, you certainly have changed since the last time," Kim commented. "Then you were ripping that envelope open in no time at all. Aren't you interested in finding out who it is anymore?"

"Oh, I think I know who it is," Emma replied breezily. She placed the vase on the end of the counter and slipped the card from its holder. Then she leaned forward for another brief, appreciative sniff.

"What?" cried Corinne.

"You know who it is?" said Kim at exactly the same instant.

Sandy looked at her curiously, while Nishiko and Mr. Jardine exchanged a grin.

"Well, I did some serious thinking over the weekend, you see," Emma told them.

"I can't stand it," Corinne cried. She had left her window and moved down the counter so that she now stood immediately behind Kim at the back of Emma's window. "If you don't open that card right this minute, I'm going to do it for you."

Emma laughed. Mr. Jardine joined in.

"So you finally figured it out, did you? I knew you would," he told her.

Corinne and Kim turned to him with equal looks of

surprise. Corinne's eyes were as wide as saucers. "You mean it *was* you?"

Mr. Jardine looked over to Emma, chuckling. "And what if it was?"

"You know I love you." Emma smiled at him, flashing her dimples.

Momentarily speechless, Corinne looked from one to the other.

Emma took pity on her and slid her fingernail beneath the flap of the envelope. She turned slightly as she lifted the card out. She didn't want Kim or Corinne to get a peek at the signature before she made the announcement. This time the surprise was for them.

"From your secret admirer," she read. Emma paused, savoring the moment. She looked up at the crowd of faces around her before lowering her eyes to the card once more. "From your secret admirer," she repeated, "and fiancé. Love, Matt."

"Matt!" Again Corinne and Kim spoke together. It was almost a shout as they exclaimed over finally learning the identity of the man they had been speculating over for the last six weeks.

"Matt!" Corinne repeated. "Who would have known?"

"Oh, I don't know," Nishiko answered. "Matt's a pretty romantic kind of guy."

Emma turned to her in surprise. Apparently she *was* the last to discover Matt's true nature. How could everyone who knew him casually realize what a handsome, romantic guy he was, while she, who knew him so well, had been oblivious?

"What's this about a fiancé?" Mr. Jardine inquired, going straight to the heart of the matter. The others had apparently overlooked the most significant word on the card. "Did you go and get yourself engaged to Matt when we weren't looking?"

Emma blushed a bright rosy pink that matched her dress to perfection. "We did have a long talk last night. After the luau. And discovered that we really do love one another. More than just as best friends," she added.

Congratulations flew in from all sides. Customers who had entered the bank while she opened the card had to be told about the latest gift. Luana was pumped for information about this last bouquet, and whether Matt had finally come into the shop himself to place the latest order.

With new incoming customers constantly needing updating, the necessity of everyone hearing personally from Emma and Luana about this latest happening, and everyone else hanging around after conducting their business, the bank had a party atmosphere for the rest of the morning. When things finally calmed down, Nishiko sent Emma and Kim off for a late lunch together.

Kim could hardly contain herself.

"I'm so happy for you I could just burst. I still can't

believe it. Not that I don't think Matt is absolutely perfect for you. That's the main reason I never went after him myself, you know."

Emma stared at her friend in amazement. "You wanted to go out with Matt, but you never did because he was my friend?"

"Well, you kept saying he was only a friend, but everybody else in town really wondered. Didn't you notice how many people guessed he was the secret admirer? But you always just pooh-poohed that and ignored it." She shook her head as she finished up her sandwich. "And I listened to you."

Emma nodded slowly. "And I appreciate you not saying 'I told you so'." Emma took a bite of her sandwich and chewed slowly. She wasn't especially hungry and was only going through the motions of eating. All she really wanted was for the day to end so that she could go home to Matt.

"It's only recently that I realized I was starting to have feelings for Matt that weren't appropriate for two good friends," she admitted. "Two platonic friends."

Kim grinned. "So. When's the wedding?"

"We talked it over last night, but we haven't decided for sure. I haven't had a chance to really talk to Mom about it yet. And I'd like Malia to come. But we want it to be soon." She cast a hopeful look at her friend. "And I want you to be my maid of honor."

"Oh, I'd love to," Kim said. "But you can't make

me wear some horrible gown," she added with a laugh. "I want veto power."

Emma cast her eyes down at her skirt, smoothing the rosy fabric. "Matt has my wedding dress all picked out."

Kim almost dropped her soda. "You're letting Matt pick your wedding dress?"

Emma smiled. "Remember the white muumuu I bought in Honolulu?"

Kim nodded. "The one you said was impractical because of the color and the train."

"Last week when I was trying to decide what to wear to the dinner on Saturday, I had Matt come over and tried on a couple of things. I ended up wearing my red muumuu to the dinner. But Matt loved the white. It was too dressy for the convention dinner party with all those people from the mainland. But Matt said it would make a beautiful wedding dress."

"Oh, Emma." Kim released her breath with a long sigh. "That is sooo romantic."

"I know." Emma put the remainder of her sandwich back in the sandwich bag. She was too happy to attempt to eat any more. "I still can't believe that I thought Matt wasn't the romantic type." She shook her head in wonder at her own stupidity. "Even after our moonlight dinner, and the rose music box . . . I just had this preconceived notion of him and of our relationship, and I didn't want to let it go." She propped her elbow on the table and rested her chin on her hand.

"He's just the nicest, kindest, most romantic man I know."

"And the hunkiest too, don't forget," Kim added.

Emma grinned. "Amen."